Fractured Vows

JESSICA AMES

FRASER CRIME SYNDICATE

FRACTURED
Vows

Author's Note

This book contains upsetting themes. For a full list of these themes visit: https://www.jessicaamesauthor.com/jessicaamestwcw

This book is set in the United Kingdom. Some spellings may differ.

CHAPTER 1

Sariah

For as long as I can remember I've dreamed of Death. He's not dressed in black, and he doesn't have a scythe either, but Death haunts my steps, following me like a rabid dog that needs to be put out of its misery. I know why Death is constantly on my mind.

Because of her.

Because of what *he* did.

Because of what I allowed.

I stare down at my hands, expecting to see red. They are clean, but I can feel the blood coating them. I kept my silence all these years and hid the truth from the world. I should have spoken up, but I was scared. That cowardice pains me more than the thought of dying.

"You say she's eighteen?"

The question breaks me from my morbid thoughts. I zone in on the man standing in front of me.

Jeremiah Wood.

Head of the Wood Syndicate.

And the man my father is forcing me to marry.

He's older, in his fifties and not unattractive, but as his

rough hand runs over my cheek I have to swallow back the bile.

"Recently turned," my father says in a detached tone.

Barely a week ago.

My birthday wasn't a celebration. There was no cake and no banners. No presents either. My father only acknowledged the day with a callous reminder that I am old enough to be married. He didn't waste any time calling this meeting to start the process of joining me to a man they call "the Butcher."

I watch as Jeremiah circles me, a vulture waiting to swoop in and devour his prey. That's what I am: a possession. An object.

Soulless.

I lost my soul when my mother was murdered. My heart still beats but I'm not alive. I haven't been from the moment my mother was murdered.

She would never have allowed him to treat me like a business deal.

She would have fought my father every step of the way.

My stomach twists as I meet my father's gaze. There's not a hint of remorse or sadness for what he's forcing me into. Whatever feelings he may have had for me in the past no longer exist and haven't since the night my mother spilt her secrets.

My father's steely eyes meet mine, unrepentant.

He doesn't care that he's selling me to a man who is old enough to be my grandfather.

He doesn't care that my body will be used and abused at Jeremiah's whims.

He doesn't care that I will be deeply unhappy.

This is the way of our world.

London is run by a number of crime families, gangs, and motorcycle clubs. There are three main families: the Eastons, the Frasers, and the Adams.

The Farleys and Blackwoods are gone, both taken out by the Untamed Sons Motorcycle Club—the former with the help of the Frasers.

My father doesn't tell me the ins and outs of his empire, the sticky, dirty secrets that weave through the complex webs they create, but I hear things. I've learnt it pays to be one step ahead and to know what's coming before it hits you between the eyes.

The only thing that matters is building alliances.

That's all I am—a bargaining chip. Giving me to Jeremiah will ensure strong ties between the Easton and the Wood syndicates. It will secure both families' futures while in turn destroying mine. I will become the ashes of the fire they light. Caught in the crossfire of whatever war they are cooking up.

Jeremiah's greedy gaze roams over my body, as if he already owns it. He's imagining the ways he's going to rip my virginity from me, I'm sure. The thought makes panic cling to my veins.

I resist the urge to recoil, knowing it will anger him and inflame my father. My clothes hide the evidence of the last beating he gave me, but the ache in my chest reminds me he has the power to hurt with more than words.

Jeremiah cups my face, turning my head this way and that, trying to get a good look at his purchase. He may not have bought me with money, but he owns me nevertheless, and I can't ever forget that. My life is not mine. I belonged first to my father, and now to Jeremiah.

I keep my expression neutral even as I scream internally. Every inch of my body feels like it's burning.

I want to retch.

Instead, I steel my spine, lift my chin a little higher and try to disappear into my head. I try to find sanctuary in the memories of my mother, of the days when my father wasn't a monster—to me at least. On some level he's always been the devil in a suit and tie, but his cruelty towards me only started when our dirty little secret was exposed. One my mother carried with her for years.

I'm not his daughter.

Declan Easton could deal with almost anything, but knowing his progeny didn't have a drop of his own blood within her shredded the last piece of humanity he had left.

He's hated me every moment since.

This is a secret he will take to the grave. No one will ever know the truth. It would weaken him if people knew he is not my father. It would make his crown slip off his head a little. How can a man rule if he can't even keep his wife in his bed?

So we perpetuate this lie. Him, to save face. Me, because it's safer to be under his care than outside of it.

"She will do," Jeremiah says finally, as if he's passing judgement on an ornament and not a person. He dips his head and presses his lips to mine.

It takes everything I have not to push him away. I endure the act without protest, but I don't reciprocate it. I'm frozen in terror that things could go further and that my father would not stop it.

Jeremiah collars the back of my neck possessively, his fingers digging into my nape so hard it makes me wince. He's claiming ownership, letting me know I am his and there is nothing I can do about it.

He deepens the kiss, his tongue sliding along the seam of my mouth, pushing, demanding entry. I don't want to give it. It's more than I can stand. I pull away, ripping my lips from his and turning my head to the side.

I feel violated.

Dirty.

And this was only a kiss.

My father moves towards us, his expression conciliatory.

"She's just shy," he tells Jeremiah even as he grabs my wrist and squeezes it so hard tears want to form in my eyes. It feels like he's trying to shatter the bone. Shatter me. "Give her a little time, and she'll warm up. The girl hasn't been around men much."

The anger clouding Jeremiah's face dissipates a little at my father's assurance that I'm not defective and that I am pure. That I do want him. Another hard squeeze to my wrist has me forcing a smile. It's a mask I hide behind. I feel the bars of the cage surrounding me, fencing me in as Jeremiah returns his attention to me. He grabs my chin, his grip bruising.

"You will be the perfect wife. I don't like to be embarrassed." I hear the unspoken threat clearly.

Be good. Toe the line or face the consequences.

I lower my eyes and nod. I hate myself for doing it. I hate the weakness I'm showing, but this is not a situation I can survive without being submissive.

Jeremiah leans into me, his mouth going to the shell of my ear as his hand cups me between my legs. My dress does nothing to protect me from his touch, and I can't stop from drawing in a breath as his fingers stroke me through my underwear. I want to shove him away. I want to make this intrusion stop, but I freeze, my brain unable to compute the violation taking place, unable to believe my father is standing there allowing this to happen.

He's not my father...

He may make you call him that, but Declan Easton is nothing to you, and you are nothing to him.

Jeremiah tears through my thoughts as he speaks into my ear. His breath is heated against my skin and it makes me tremble with terror. "Your pussy belongs to me. I'm going to enjoy being the first man in your cunt." He rubs me harder and a thousand thoughts collide in my brain. Nausea climbs up my throat and I feel rooted to the ground. This is a dream. A bad dream.

But I'm not waking up.

My heart is pounding in time with the roaring in my ears. I want to fight. I want to stop this, but I'm no match for two grown men who will put a bullet in me if I don't do as I'm told.

I know this because my father ended my mother's life for her betrayal. He killed her and he covered it up. Men like him get away with murder and there's nothing anyone can do. Justice is an elusive concept in my world. There's only blood and destruction. There are only winners and losers. People like me don't come out on top. We fall with the rest of the pawns on the chessboard while the kings watch safely from their towers built of ivory.

My father denies he killed her, of course he does, but I know the truth. He loved my mother before her indiscretion. Loved her like she was his reason for breathing. That he was so easily able to steal her life tells me he would have no issue doing the same to me.

Because Declan Easton—the only father I've ever known—does not love me.

Maybe he did once, and it's that hope I hold on to. I'm still the little girl in the pale pink dress trying to get her father's attention, even though I know he will never give it to me. In reality I am a dirty secret. I don't know why he didn't kill me too.

Some days I wish he had.

Jeremiah pulls back a little and scans my eyes. The dark storm clouds that swirl in his gaze terrify me. They hint at the monster he is and at the horror my life is about to become. Life with my father has been difficult, but Jeremiah means to own me body and soul.

"The wedding will take place in four weeks' time," he tells

me. "I wanted sooner, but that's the quickest it can be done." A shiver runs up my spine, icy claws clutching at my heart. It takes everything in me not to pull away as he takes his hand from between my legs and brushes my hair off my face, as if he didn't just violate me.

Four weeks.

That's the only reprieve I get.

"You really are very beautiful, Sariah." He leans forward and I steel myself, thinking he's about to kiss me again. He does, but this time he brushes his lips over my cheek. I shudder internally.

"Until we meet again," he says.

He pulls back and I stand frozen to the spot as he goes to my father. They talk for a moment, though I have no idea what they say. My mind is locked on what happened. My skin slithers with disgust. I feel like a thousand ants are climbing over me.

I barely register the door opening and then closing again. I remain transfixed in the spot Jeremiah left me in.

My soon-to-be husband.

My mouth tastes like ash.

Without warning my father slams his hand around my throat. He pushes me back so my spine hits the plasterwork behind me. My feet scramble to keep upright and it's only his hold on me that keeps me from falling on my face.

He tightens his grip on my neck, and with nowhere to go, I do the only thing I can to relieve the pressure. I lift my head, which exposes the soft underside of my throat even more.

"Do you enjoy embarrassing me?" he demands. "He owns you! Every part of you, Sariah. You have no right to pull away from him!"

He will have expected me to bow and scrape to Jeremiah, act like the dutiful wife-to-be. His eyes blaze as he takes me in, spittle collecting at the sides of his mouth. I've seen him angry more times than I can count over the years. His rage is quick to blow and slow to die down. Like a volcano, his temper is explosive.

He's glaring at me like wants to squeeze the life out of me. I should feel terror at that, but I'm not afraid to die. Living is more terrifying than any end my father could give me.

His fingers are like vices, crushing my windpipe. My survival instinct kicks in, a desperate need to live, even if my head wants to be put out of its misery. I jolt back, trying to move his hand. When that doesn't work, I claw at his hand. My nails rake over his skin and his blood bubbles up. He doesn't even register my attempts to free myself. My eyes find his and all I see reflected back at me is pure hate.

He slams his fist into my side hard enough that white spots dance across my vision even as the edges are starting to darken. My ribs protest, pain radiating out like an atomic blast from the site of impact. He releases his hold on my throat so that I can suck in a breath.

Turning me, he shoves me against the wall, pressing my face into the plaster, his chest to my back. His weight constricts my lungs, stopping my chest from moving to draw in air. "You will marry Jeremiah Wood. You will protect this family's name, and you will be a dutiful fucking wife. You owe me this much."

Fear keeps my words lodged in my throat. My father is a killer and I'm in his hands. He releases me and storms from the room. I stay locked in position, listening to his retreating footsteps before the door opens and slams shut. I don't let the tears fall, even though they want to.

Carefully, I push away from the wall and move over to the sofa. Bruised and shattered, I sink gingerly onto it, holding my aching ribs, my heart racing in my chest.

I will marry Jeremiah. I will walk down that aisle in front of the hundreds of people and I will plaster a fake smile on my face, because what other choice is there? If I refuse my father will kill me, and while I dream of death, I'm not sure I covet it. I want freedom, not an end to my life. I want to live without the cage keeping me captive. I want to travel. I want to see the world. I want to experience things other normal teenagers do.

I want my decisions to be my own.

Jeremiah thinks he will be the first man between my legs?

No.

If that monster thinks he's getting my virginity, he's wrong. It seems like such a small thing to care about, but I have to fight the battles I can. This is something I can control. I would rather let a stranger fuck me than suffer the indignity of my first time with a man I despise. At least it will be on my terms then. At least I will have the ability to choose.

I just have to find someone.

And fast.

Because in four weeks' time, my life will be controlled completely by Jeremiah Wood, and I get the feeling he is a worst beast than my father.

CHAPTER 2

Lucas

The blood drips off the knife. It glistens in the light, a macabre reminder of the life I've just taken, while the coppery smell of it lingers in the air, choking my lungs.

I peer up at the body. His head hangs low between his shoulders, his strung-up arms the only thing keeping him upright. If it wasn't for the chains around his torn-up bloodied wrists, he'd be a heap on the floor. He is gone.

I scan his body, looking at my handiwork. Slashes and cuts litter his torso, his skin reddened where I'd burnt the flesh with lighters and cigarettes. Teeth and fingernails are scattered on the concrete beneath him while trails of crimson flow from the slash across his throat and the stab wounds to his belly. It creates a ruby waterfall. The human body is an amazing feat of biology, but it's fragile too. I'd pushed this cunt to his limits and beyond.

Hours of torture. Hours of fun.

"You done?" Zeke demands, his voice irritated. My brother is a changed man since he married his woman, Bailey. He wants to get home to his family. He still has that thirst for blood, but it doesn't consume him in the same way as it does Kane and me. I need to let my demons out, need to feed them, and bloodletting is the only way to do that.

"I'm done," I say. Glancing back at the corpse, I commit every slice, cut, and inch of damage to memory before I pull my lips together and spit on the dead man. "Fucking cunt."

He is—or was—a member of the West Lake gang, a bunch of small-time crooks who think they are more important than they are. They run around the city, acting like they rule the fucking roost.

They couldn't be more wrong.

They can't be the big men when they're nothing but vermin.

I will tear anyone apart who tries to take my family down. My family—the Frasers—own a small section of London that encompasses part of Clerkenwell. In the past six months the West Lake gang intercepted a shipment of drugs, helped by one of our supposedly loyal men. We'd retaliated for that offence. We'd killed at least half a dozen of their men and left their mutilated corpses for them to find. It was a message. A strong one. It should have been the end of it, but these fuckers are stupid and reckless. The latest crap they are pulling is scaring local businesses to pay them for protection —businesses that already pay us. My father is going to have to act soon to take these fuckers down. It's humiliating.

"They're getting brazen," Zeke notes, pushing off the wall. His eyes blaze with anger, little pyres burning brightly as he takes in the body of the man I tortured to death. There's no remorse or sympathy for that fucker. He got what he deserved.

Zeke smooths his dark grey suit down. It is tailored exactly to his frame, and he has quality Italian leather shoes on his feet that cost more than most people's rent. I know because I'm wearing the same designer. His hair is brushed back off his forehead and he's got a couple days' worth of growth on his face. He looks more like a Wall Street banker than a mobster.

"This shit has got to stop," he snarls. I understand his frustration. It's pissing me off too.

The sound of his feet scraping across the concrete echoes around the kill room as he comes away from the body and steps towards me. The acoustics are fucking phenomenal in here. When a man is screaming and begging for his life, the way it reverberates around the space is the sweetest symphony on the planet.

"Preaching to the fucking choir, brother," I mutter, moving to the sink.

I grab a wash cloth and rinse it under the tap. The cold water wakes me up a little, pulling me out of the killing haze that has consumed me for the past few hours. My head feels fucking fuzzy, like I'm drunk on the bloodlust.

I wipe across my bare chest, which is splattered with red droplets, cleaning every hint of evidence of the murder I have committed from my skin. It doesn't matter. I still have the memories of what I did. Those are emblazoned on my mind, a movie reel of horror that I get off on. I am a monster hidden behind a suit and tie, and I'm unapologetic about the fact. I would kill a thousand men if it keeps my family safe.

"I would prefer not to go to war," Zeke says, "but if that's what it's going to take to make these cunts back down, I'm all for it."

"Try telling that to Anthony." I don't have the will to refer to the man as "Father." He's certainly never been that to us.

I dry myself off, letting the rough towel scrape over skin that feels too sensitive. My whole body feels wired and alert.

Alive.

I always feel the same way after a kill. Most people would feel each murder chip away at their humanity. Not me. I never felt a moment of regret or remorse for the lives I've taken.

"How are the girls and Bailey?"

Zeke cocks a brow at me. "There's a dead man hanging a foot from us and you want to make small talk?"

I smirk at him. "It's not like he's listening."

He lets out a snort of laughter. Zeke is the easiest of my siblings. Kane is hot-headed and quick to anger, and even Aurelia, our sister, can be difficult. She has our mother's temperament at times and can be a raging fucking bitch when she feels like it. I feel for the man our parents will give her to.

"It feels like this is the only time I get to talk to you." I sound sullen, like a little boy who is missing his big brother.

It's not a lie. Zeke is wrapped up in his life, and I don't begrudge him that. He deserves every ounce of goodness he has.

His wife has made some of the darkness in his eyes dim down. Zeke's not as hard as he was. Some of those sharp edges have been smoothed away. The blackness that shrouds him—shrouds all of us—will never completely go, but he has something to live for now. He has a family to protect.

As well as Bailey, Zeke has two stepdaughters, Kara and Mollie. They're sweet girls, untouched by the horrors their world is surrounded by. Neither Zeke nor Bailey let the filth of what we do sully them. Bailey grew up in the Untamed Sons, a motorcycle club that we're now allied with. She knows the shit we do and she knows how bad it can get. She was sold through a trafficking ring by one of our enemies. Luckily Zeke was the one who bought her. Things hadn't gone exactly to plan. He was supposed to hand her back to the Sons. Instead, my crazy brother took Bailey home with him. It nearly caused a war. It probably would have done if the two of them hadn't fallen in love. Bailey went through a lot at the hands of her captors. Zeke has done what he can to help her, but those scars will never fully heal. They never do.

So I don't blame them for keeping those girls in the dark. They're young, with their lives ahead of them. They have the chance to break free of the chains that bind the rest of us. I wish our mother had done more to protect us growing up. Instead she stood at our father's side, the queen to his king, pulling strings behind the scenes and making Anthony dance like a fucking marionette. Their actions left us this way.

Broken.

Cold.

Ruthless.

Our parents have a reputation of their own. Anthony Fraser is the man who stole his own brother's bride and then killed him savagely. He'd committed fratricide to have our mother. He'd thrown the whole family into civil war. From the stories I've heard, it was a merciless battle, one that our father won by the skin of his teeth. He and Charlotte were given their throne along with the keys to the kingdom, and they've ruled it ever since. My brothers and I are just pawns on their chessboard, moved wherever suits the needs of the family—or the firm, as it's also known.

I reach for my shirt where it's hanging on a hook on the wall and shrug into it.

"You're fucking tapped in the head," Zeke tells me, leaning against the wall next to the sink. "But they're all fine. Bailey wants you to come over for dinner when you're free next."

That's not happening. I like my sister-in-law, would lay down my life to protect her and those kids, but playing house is not my thing. "Maybe another time," I say.

Zeke's brows draw together. "It's dinner, not a fucking execution."

"I'd be willing to go if it was."

He grabs my bicep, his hold firm but not tight. "Don't make me disappoint my fucking wife," he hisses at me.

I finish buttoning my shirt and grab my suit jacket off the same hook. "You know all that domestic shit isn't my thing."

"It's one dinner, Lucas. You'll fucking survive. Kane and Aurelia will be there."

That makes me pause. Kane would never agree to this kind of shit. He hates organised fun more than I do. "Kane said yes?"

"I haven't asked him yet," he admits.

I huff out a breath as I settle my suit in place. It feels like putting my armour on, a defence against the world.

"If he says yes, I'll come," I compromise, knowing Kane will never agree.

Zeke clearly also knows it, because his lips pull into a tight line. "Just come and don't be a dick." He turns back to the body and waves a hand in its direction. "You got a clean-up crew for this?"

"I'll sort one." I follow Zeke out of the building, leaving our friend hanging like a pig from the hook. As I walk out, I fire a text off to the men who will make this shit disappear as if we were never here. We pay them premium rates to ensure no evidence is left behind—including the body.

Illuminated in the headlights, Ryan Malone, Zeke's body-guard, and Nick Winters, my own personal security, are leaning against the Bentley. Zeke's black Audi is parked behind it. Neither car is conspicuous if the police happened to pass, but the building is off the beaten track. It's deep within an industrial estate that was abandoned by the businesses during the 2008 global recession. The whole site is empty. Streets filled with warehouses and units without occupants.

An industrial graveyard.

We bought the whole lot a couple of years back. We'll

never sell a single unit. It's too useful to us for hiding the shittier parts of our empire—like torturing and murdering our enemies.

Ryan's eyes roam over Zeke, checking to see that he's whole. When he's satisfied, he relaxes a little, some of that ramrod tension leaving his spine and shoulders. He's a big fucking guy, former Special Forces, and has been with Zeke for the past four years now. I like him. He cares about my brother, and that means he's likely to keep him breathing.

Winters, on the other hand, puts me on fucking edge. He used to be my mother's guard until my father suspected things were happening between them. I'd like to think my mother wouldn't cheat on the man who killed to have her, but if it furthered one of her schemes, I doubt there's a line she wouldn't cross. I don't know why my father didn't kill Winters—he should have—but the whole situation makes me distrust the fucker.

Zeke stops walking. "Come to dinner, Luke. Make my wife happy."

"I thought that was your job."

"Lucas." The warning snaps through his tone. Usually, I'd ignore it, but I'm riding the high from my kill and I want to keep it.

"Fine. I'll come to fucking dinner."

Zeke smirks as if he's won some great prize. Fucker. "I'll let Bailey know."

I mutter a curse under my breath as my phone buzzes to let me know the clean-up crew are on their way.

"You good waiting?" he asks.

I nod. "Yeah. Get going."

I watch as Zeke walks over to his car with Ryan and gets in. As they drive away, I climb in the back of the Bentley while Winters climbs in the front. I scroll through my messages, answering a few emails for some of our legitimate businesses before the cleaners turn up.

As soon as they do, I order Winters to drive me back to my place. After a kill there's only one thing I want to do.

Fuck.

I need to release all this fucking pressure in my body.

I head up to my apartment and take a shower. As soon as I'm clean, I pull on a fresh pair of trousers and a dark shirt. Then I head into the city to one of the local bars I like to go to.

The firm owns a few clubs and bars in our slice of London, but I avoid those, and for good reason.

My mother's little spies.

They are everywhere, feeding back to her every morsel of dirty information they can.

Winters is waiting when I step out of the lift. He doesn't bother asking where we're going. He knows my routine well enough to know I need to get lost for a few hours.

We head to the car in the parking garage. I climb in the back as he gets in the driver's seat. I glance at him in the rear-view mirror. I suspect this fucker has my mother in his ear, and that he's feeding her shit about me. Those thoughts are like poison spreading through me, a paranoia I can't control.

He stops outside Tease, a club that has become my home away from home. We both climb out and he hands the car keys to the valet before following me to the front of the line where there are girls waiting in barely-there skirts and tops that reveal expanses of flesh. They shiver against the cold, but they aren't wearing coats. There are guys in shirts and trousers, their hair slicked back. They'll be in the toilets as soon as they get inside, doing lines of that magic white powder or dropping uppers. Getting out of their heads long enough to forget about their miserable lives for just a few hours.

17

The bouncer, a mountain of a man with a shaved head and thick moustache, lets me bypass the queue to go inside. These fuckers all know who I am and what I'm capable of. It makes them bend over backwards to be accommodating.

Inside the club, the music is loud, the bass vibrating through the floor. The smell of sweat and booze clings to the air, infusing my nose as I make my way to the bar. I can feel Winters watching me, but he doesn't follow too closely, giving me space to fucking breathe.

I get a drink at the bar, keeping my eye on two blonde women standing at the other end. They're fucking gorgeous and they keep giving me fuck-me eyes. Maybe I can convince them both to come to a hotel with me. It's been a while since I played double tag.

I let my gaze roam around the club. The flashing strobe lights illuminate the dance floor in pulsing waves, giving tantalising views of the women here tonight. Taking a sip of my drink, I watch the gyrating mass of bodies as they sway back and forth with the music. Tease stocks my choice of Scotch exclusively for me. It's not like I would throw a hissy fit if they didn't have it, but they think I will lose my shit and make the bar run with blood.

Better to keep people on their fucking toes and guessing what I might do than let them think otherwise.

Better to keep that fear burrowing deep inside them, making them pliable and willing.

Fear is the best kind of weapon. It allows doubts to grow. It allows those little niggling feelings to spread like a cancer through every cell in your body. I know how to deliver it in order to expose people's worst fears. It's a skill that runs deep and allows me to control those around me—like my mother does. Knowing that makes me feel fucking sick to my stomach. She's the last person I'd want to emulate.

I take another sip of my drink, relishing the burn of the

alcohol as it hits the back of my throat. I am about to give my attention back to the blondes when I see her.

She's tiny, maybe five three or four, and she's wearing a white summer dress that makes her stand out. She looks like a white rose among a stem full of thorns. The animals in this club would prick her and make her bleed if I let them touch her. She's got blonde hair that trails down her back in natural waves, and her eyes dart around like she's seeing everything for the first time.

I follow her through the crowd of people, keeping my distance but staying close enough to intercede if—if what? I have no fucking idea. All I know is that dead lump of meat that sits in my chest just gave a lub-dub for the first time in years.

CHAPTER 3

Sariah

A club isn't my scene, especially one called Tease, but it's close to home, and in truth it was the first place I came across that didn't look sleazy. I'd rather have my head stuck in a book than find myself pressed within a mass of sweaty bodies, but I'm set on going through with my plan. I'm going to lose my virginity on my terms. When Jeremiah touched me without my permission, it left me feeling filthy, like I was covered in dirt that no shower would ever scrub clean. Even the thought of getting naked with the man makes my skin crawl as if a thousand fire ants are walking over me. I don't want my first time to be with him.

I'm shoved roughly to the side and into a large man with a faux hawk as the crowd swells and moves like a living breathing thing. I feel like a ship tossed at sea, and I try to keep my legs beneath me as I move with the wave of people. My heart is hammering in my chest, fear making me twitchy and uneasy. I've never been anywhere on my own before. There is always security following me. I'm starting to realise the gravity of my mistake. I'm not used to this level of freedom, and I feel exposed, torn open, ripped apart. It makes heat sear through my veins.

Getting out of the house had not been easy. My father has guards on me twenty-four seven. I had to wait until the whole household had gone to bed and then sneak out of my window. Getting past the layers of security surrounding the perimeter of the house should have been tricky, but I know their routines. I knew where they would be and where there would be gaps in their security. I know everything about that house because it has been my prison for the past eighteen years.

My upcoming nuptials have made me defiant in a way I have never been.

Because I fear the alternative more.

I fear what Jeremiah will do to me the night of our wedding. I have no idea where this sudden strength has come from. I have never possessed it before. Usually, I toe the line. I do what is expected of me. I'm so frightened of my father and his iron fist I have never dared to step out against him. I know what defying him leads to. The bruises that cover my body rarely heal before new ones are given, but desperation drove me to this. I feel the abject panic of the clock ticking down with every waking moment. In less than a month's time I will be married, and all my choices will disappear the moment that ring shackles me to Jeremiah.

I want to make my own decisions and be in charge of my destiny. I know I can't stop the wedding. To even attempt it would be suicide. If my father didn't kill me, Jeremiah would. The shame it would bring to his family name if I refused to walk down the aisle would be greater than any shame he would feel about taking my life. As important as I am for building alliances, I am also disposable. Women have little place in our life, and I am no different.

As I glance around at the scantily clad women and the men who are dressed to party, I feel out of my depth. It's like murky waters are settling around my neck, threatening to drown me in its swells. This is a surreal dream. I can't decide if it's a nightmare or not.

I feel a hand slide onto my bottom, and I can't stop from squeaking in surprise. I twist around and see a cheeky-looking man giving me a smirk. "Fancy a fuck?"

The brazenness of his words takes me aback. Never before has a man spoken to me in such harsh and forward terms—other than Jeremiah, but he bought and paid for me. Others wouldn't dare. My father would gut them for such disrespect. He may not respect me, but he certainly respects the Easton name, and he will at least do what he has to on the surface in order to protect my honour while we still perpetuate the lie that I am his daughter.

I stumble back from the man, falling into another who grabs me by the elbows to steady me. I pull away, my skin feeling hot where he touched me, and not in a nice way. It feels raw and wrong, like flames licking up my arm.

The man holding me smirks, a macabre look that makes my stomach roil. "What is a pretty thing like you doing here on your own?"

I try to pull back, but he doesn't release his iron grip on me. I shove him roughly, but he barely moves an inch. His eyes are wide, wired and he has a wild look that instantly makes all my instincts snap to alert.

"Let go of me!" I hiss. I'm not sure if he can hear me over the steady bass that is thumping through the massive speakers on either side of the stage, so I give him another push.

"We're just having fun, sweetheart." He grins at me, but I'm not having fun at all. Fear is galloping through my veins, leaving icy crystals in its wake, and my stomach is churning savagely, making me feel nauseous.

Just as my panic starts to take hold, a hand reaches over me and grabs the man's wrist. He does something, a movement I barely register, but the man releases his hold on me with a scream of pain.

"She said no," a silky-smooth voice says from over my shoulder.

I twist around and peer up at my saviour. He's not the white knight on the horse. He is the black robed horsemen coming to claim my soul. When I look in his eyes, I see nothing there but swirling darkness. I should be afraid—terrified—and part of me is, but I'm also enthralled. There is something about him that draws my attention like the moth to the flame. I know I will get burned, but right now that seems irrelevant.

Every inch of my body feels lit up. It's like the air around me is so thin I can hardly draw in oxygen. My lungs stutter as my heart skips a beat. I've never felt a visceral reaction to a man before, but whoever he is, he makes me feel like I'm drowning on land. I swallow back my fear, but the man has eyes for no one but my attacker. He shoves him back ruthlessly, doing with one hand what I had attempted to do with both. The man who grabbed me goes down, taking two other people with him as he sprawls on the ground. The sound of shattering glass fills the air, loud even over the sound of the music.

My saviour gives me his attention and I get lost in his gaze. I can't tell what colour his eyes are in the flashing strobe lights of the club, but they appeared to be almost black.

He doesn't say a word. He holds his hand out to me, a poisoned olive branch. I know I shouldn't take it, that I should run far and fast from this man, but my hand slips into his. Danger hasn't just come knocking—it's broken down the door and is staring me in the face, taunting me. Laughing at me.

The crowd of people part like the Red Sea as he turns and walks me back towards the bar area. He walks past a large security guard, who looks like he could break my neck with his bare hands, and pushes through a door that is marked VIP. I should stop this. I should pull away, but my hand is cemented to his.

The music is a dull thud as the door shuts behind us and the fluorescent lights blind me momentarily. I blink against the brightness and try to see where I am. I'm greeted by a long corridor with whitewashed walls. I instantly realise the danger I'm in. I tug my hand back, making him stop in his tracks. He turns towards to me and I get a good look at him.

He steals my breath. I know it's not right to call a man beautiful, but there is no other word to describe his perfection. I have never seen a man as beautiful as he is. His eyes are not in fact black as I thought them to be when we were on the main floor of the club but a tantalising blue that reminds me of the ocean. The colour looks peaceful on the surface, but dangers are hidden underneath, and I suspect the same is true of this man. He has short sandy-blond hair and a layer of light scruff covers his face. There is no warmth in his eyes.

"What are you doing here?" he asks, as if he understands I have no business being in a place like this.

Since I can't tell him the truth, I murmur, "I needed a distraction."

"I can help you with that."

He backs me up against the wall, pressing his body against mine. My heart starts to race, and my chest starts to heave as the air suddenly feels thin.

I meet his eyes and I get lost in their turbulence. He snags my chin, forcing my attention back to him. His fingers leave trails of fire where he touches my skin, and I feel too hot.

"What's your name?" he demands.

I don't answer. I can't. My tongue is glued to the roof of my mouth. Everything about this man exudes danger, and I'm drawn to it.

"Name," he repeats.

"Alice," I say quietly, giving him my mother's name. Something tells me I need to protect my identity, especially from a man who looks like this.

He gives me a smile that touches his eyes, chasing the demons away for just a moment. "Well, Alice, I'm about to give you the best night of your fucking life."

CHAPTER 4

Lucas

The pretty little thing in front of me is a delectable bite. Her gaze darts around making her seem like a frightened rabbit.

I like the virginal vibe she's giving off. It's so different from the normal skanks and whores who frequent these clubs. There's no shortage of women throwing themselves at my feet. They see the suit and the suaveness, and they assume I have money. It's only when they look into my eyes and they see the evil within me that they back off. At least, most do; some like danger—crave it, even. I can relate because I am the same. I enjoy the thrill of the chase, the adrenaline rush of doing things that make my heart race.

Dipping my head, I press a kiss to the side of Alice's neck. I know it's not her real name. She didn't say it like she owned it, but I don't give a fuck why she's lying. I just want to get into her knickers.

She sucks in a breath and stiffens, going as rigid as a board. It makes me pause. I don't think she's unwilling, just nervous.

"Relax." I brush my lips against the softness of her skin,

smelling strawberries as I do. This girl not only looks like an angel but she also smells like heaven.

"You... you didn't... tell me your name," she says breathlessly. I don't answer. I just keep kissing along her neckline. "I really think... I should know your name."

"You're talking too much," I warn her.

She huffs out of breath at my tone, which melts into a moan as I hit a spot that seems particularly sensitive. I let my hand roam and find her tit. I give it a squeeze. I'm not gentle, though I don't go as hard as I would with someone else. She's got that untouched quality to her, but people who come to Tease aren't innocent wallflowers. It makes me wonder if this is an act.

Then again, who comes to a club wearing a summer dress?

She starts to speak again, and I close my mouth over hers, silencing her. I don't want chit-chat. I want someone to fuck.

I lick my tongue along the seam of her mouth and she opens hesitantly. It's all the invitation I need. I lick inside, finding her tongue and caressing it with mine. She tastes sweet, and I can't place what she's been drinking.

I keep one hand wrapped around her breast while I dip the other under her dress and find her underwear. She's soaked. It makes me want to beat my chest like a fucking savage.

I slide her underwear aside and slip a finger into her tight hole. Alice clamps her thighs together instantly, trying to stop my intrusion. "This is moving too fast," she mumbles.

But it's not moving fast enough.

I need more. I want to lift that dress up and feast on her pussy, but I like a bitch to be willing.

"You want to stop?" I ask.

She peers into my eyes. I watch as she pulls her bottom lip between her teeth, her expression uncertain. Is she about to disappoint me? "No." She sounds breathy as she speaks the word.

I give her a smirk. Thank fuck for that. She unclamps her thighs and I push two fingers inside her. I force them deep inside her tight channel. She gasps and tenses at first. I consider stopping for a fleeting moment, but I feel her start to loosen as her pleasure starts to build. She grips my biceps, her nails digging in hard enough to leave half-moons in my skin. I don't pay any attention. All I care about is what is going to come.

Alice keeps her eyes locked on my face, and intensity flickers beneath the surface of her fear. I rub my thumb over her clit and her head tips back as she gasps out an uncontrollable moan. Yeah, she is an angel. I want to spread her on my bed and feast on her pussy like a starved man.

My thoughts scatter as I feel her tighten around me, pulsating and contracting as her orgasm hits.

She lets out a shuddering cry that goes straight to my balls, making my cock stiffen in my trousers. The need to be inside her is growing. I should take her here and now, shove her dress up and thrust inside her. I've done it hundreds of times before with other women, but this is different. From what I can see, Alice is not like those girls. I don't want anyone to witness what we're about to do. For some reason, I feel the need to protect her from prying eyes. I want Alice to myself, and I'm not willing to share her.

Regretfully, I pull my fingers out of her.

She peers up at me with wide dazed eyes as I suck her juices off my fingers. Her cheeks turn pink.

"Have I embarrassed you, little dove?" I'm amused. The women I sleep with aren't usually so coy.

"No."

Liar.

I stroke a finger under her chin like she's a lazy cat in need of taming. "I don't believe you," I tell her in a soft voice.

I take her hand and I pull her towards the exit. I want somewhere private where I can fuck her properly. She stumbles after me, her heels clacking against the tile beneath our feet.

"Where are we going?" she asks in a small voice.

I don't answer. I need her now. My dick feels like a rock growing steadily harder by the second.

I push through the door that leads into the VIP section. The light is poor in here, just like in the club. There are no strobes, but there are dimly lit wall lights. They barely cast enough glow to see what we're doing.

Clutching her hand, I drag her over to the Staff Only entrance and step through into another corridor. It's light and quiet. A complete change from the environment we just left.

I lead her into Tommy's office and flick the lights on. It's empty, which isn't surprising. Tommy, the club's owner, tends to stick close to the main floor, keeping an eye on his girls and the patrons. Trouble isn't that unusual in the club. Bitches OD'ing in the bathroom on Ecstasy and other cocktails of drugs has happened more times than I can fucking count.

I lead Alice over to the beat-up sofa pushed against the wall and come down on top of her as I push her onto it. She feels soft beneath me, and I grind my cock against her core, giving her a tantalising hint of what is to come.

"Oh!" she gasps.

My mouth finds the dip in her neck between her shoulder, sucking up the skin there as I slip a hand under the neckline of her dress and find her nipple. I rub it, rolling the bud between my fingers.

"I need to know your name," she tells me around a moan.

"Luke." I gave her the nickname my siblings use for me. I don't know why. No one else would dare call me that, but I'm giving this stranger permission to use something personal to me.

"Do you think we should slow down?"

I lean up on my palms so I can look into her face. There's no fear in her eyes, but there is something else I can't place. "Why?"

"I've… I've never done this before."

The admission doesn't shock me. I hoped she would have some experience though. I'm not looking to break anyone in.

"You're a virgin." I can't stop the hint of irritation from bleeding into my voice.

She nods, her cheeks flushing. I've fucked a lot of women over the years, lost count of how many, but I've never been someone's first. Not fucking sure how I feel about the idea either.

I'm not a man who attaches sentimentality to shit, so I don't give a fuck she's a virgin, but I do care that this isn't going to be good—for either of us. No one's first time is fireworks and fucking rainbows. It's messy, sloppy, and awkward even when you care about the person you're with. From a selfish perspective, this is going to be shit for me. I need to release my pent-up frustration. I need to fuck someone hard and fast. I can't do that with Alice. I can't drill a woman who has never been touched before.

My dick starts to soften as I come to the realisation this isn't happening tonight. Not with her. I don't want to be anyone's first.

Maybe those blondes will still be waiting at the bar…

I push up off her and stand at the edge of the sofa as I tuck my shirt back into my trousers, attempting to tidy myself up.

"That's it? I tell you I'm a virgin and you run?" She comes up on her elbows and I can see by the tight set of her jaw that I've pissed her off.

"I want to fuck, little dove. I can't fuck you."

"Why not?"

"You're a virgin," I say as if it's the most obvious thing on the planet.

"So? As far as I know I work perfectly fine... down there."

I snort a laugh. "You can't even say the word 'pussy.'"

She wrinkles her nose. "I can."

I give her my full attention. "I want to pound into your cunt. I want to have you screaming my name when I destroy your pretty little pussy. You will feel me for days, Alice, if I fuck you. That shouldn't be your first time. Find a nice boy who will make it special for you."

I'm a monster, but I'm not a dick. This girl exudes an innocence I've never seen before. It's rare in my world. Most of the women are used up, tormented, broken by the life we lead. While I'm drawn to her innocence, I'm also not going to have her first time be in Tommy's disgusting office.

Alice surprises me as anger flashes in her eyes. The fire interests me more than I care to admit.

"Fuck you," she growls, pushing off the sofa and straightening her clothes. Her movements are jerky and she refuses to meet my eyes as she puts her tits back into the cups of her bra.

I cock a brow at the vitriol spewing from her mouth. I didn't expect it, but I like that it's there. I don't like someone to be a fucking pushover. "Babe, don't make this harder than it has to be."

Angry eyes meet mine. "Am I that repulsive that you can't bring yourself to sleep with me?"

"Not at all." She's fucking gorgeous, and I'm not sure she knows it, which adds to the appeal.

"So I'm a virgin. It doesn't mean I can't do it," Alice says as she gets in my face, and I realise I've underestimated her.

She's not this innocent flower I thought she was. The woman has a temper.

"Goodbye, Alice." My tone is firm. This has gone too far. I need to stop it now before things happen that can't be undone. I'm not sure when the fuck I developed a conscience, but I can't bring myself to take her. She's not like the other bitches I surround myself with. She hasn't been tainted yet. It feels criminal to touch Alice.

She grabs my wrist, stopping me from leaving. I could easily pull free, but I don't. Instead, I turn to face her, letting my confusion bleed onto my face. There's a desperation in her eyes that puts me on edge.

"Please."

"You want to tell me why it's so important to lose your virginity here and now?"

Her eyes don't waver from mine. "I never said it was important."

"You didn't have to. I can tell."

"Fine, if you're not going to do it, I'll find someone else."

Her words piss me off. I growl under my breath. I don't know why, but the thought of someone else touching her makes red film my vision. Images of someone else between her legs, tasting that pretty pussy of hers dance across my mind.

Fuck. No.

I put a hand against the door, stopping her from opening it.

Alice peers up at me, her mouth pulled into a tight line. "Move."

"No."

"Luke—"

"Little dove, there are better ways to lose your virginity than in some back room on a dirty sofa."

The heavy look in her eyes and the dare in her expression twist me up inside.

"So show me."

Fuck, my dick hardens in my trousers as I stare down at her. All that blonde hair and those big expressive fucking eyes... My cock wants her even as my head tells me this is a bad idea. "You're going to do this no matter what."

She nods. I curse under my breath. I should let her go so she can find someone else, but I can't. Not when the thought of another man touching her makes an irrational rage grow within me. The strength of emotion surprises me because I've never felt shit for anyone outside of my family before, but she's a rose among a field of weeds. If I let her go, she'll be swallowed up by the foliage. I can't allow that to happen. "Follow me."

I don't give her the chance to say no. I take her hand in mine. When I step out of the office, Winters is waiting at the end of the corridor. He doesn't let a single emotion slide onto his face as he follows us back out into the club. The music is loud, but I focus on her hand in mine. She feels small, vulnerable. She's trembling against me as we step outside into the cooler air.

The three of us wait for the valet to bring the car back around. She eyes Winters curiously but doesn't ask about him. When the car roars up to the pavement, Winters climbs in the front while Alice and I get in the back.

Winters glances at me in the rear-view mirror, looking for directions.

"Viewpoint," I tell him.

He doesn't react. I've been to the hotel many times with many different women. Alice is a notch in a long line of other notches. She doesn't feel like that though. She feels like something more. I'm doing her a fucking service by stopping someone else from taking her. At least with me she'll get a good fucking night out of it.

Winters stops the car outside the front entrance of the hotel and climbs out. He heads inside to rent a room for us. Alice peers out of the side window and I can see how nervous she is.

When Winters returns to the car, I grab her hand and pull her out of the vehicle. Winters hands me a key card and I see the first hint of disapproval flash across his face.

Judgy prick.

Considering his past, he's got no fucking room to talk.

I lead Alice into the building and to the lift with Winters following after us. We head to the sixth floor and make our way to the room. The corridors are bright, airy, and quiet, too, given the late hour. When we reach the right room number, I slide the card into the key slot and the green light flashes. I step back and let Winters enter first. He checks the room is safe and then comes back to the door. He gives me a nod before he moves to wait in the corridor where he'll stay all night.

Stepping inside the hotel room, I hold the door open for Alice, who moves deeper inside. There's a large bed against one wall, pristine white sheets on the bed, a desk against one wall, and a love seat in the window. It's clean, and luxurious as fuck.

Usually, the women I bring here have a reaction to seeing the room for the first time. Surprisingly, Alice doesn't. Her gaze skims her surroundings before coming back to me.

Fuck, I can't believe I'm going to do this shit.

CHAPTER 5

Sariah

My heart is pounding so hard Luke must be able to hear it. This is what I wanted. This is why I'm here, but standing in a hotel room about to let a man in between my legs has my body shaking.

I'm an Easton—in name, at least. Showing fear is a weakness I'm not allowed to have, so I steel my spine and move to the bed. I have to do this. It needs to be on my terms. Jeremiah won't make it easy for me. He'll use me hard and fast, and he'll shatter me. Though I don't think Luke will be any easier on me. He looks like a man built to destroy.

Swallowing hard, I sink onto the edge of the bed, skimming my hands over the covers.

He watches me as I slip my dress off my shoulders. The material pools around my waist, revealing my lace-covered breasts. Fumbling, I unhook my bra and let it fall free. I choke down my anxiety as his gaze drops to my tits.

"Fuck," he mutters.

My cheeks heat at his tone. There is so much desire in that one little word that it makes my belly flip. He wants me, and not because of who I am or what I can do for him. He wants me because he likes what he sees. That realisation is heady, and it makes me feel elated.

I have no idea what I'm doing, but I've watched movies. When I was at school, I saw what the girls did with the boys. My school friends talked about their escapades. I wish I had friends now, but my father keeps me isolated from everyone. Leaving school was the worst thing that happened to me because now I'm truly alone.

I take one of my breasts in my hand and gently squeeze it. I've never done anything so erotic, and I feel slutty. Luke seems to like it, because his eyes are molten. It's like liquid courage, seeing that expression directed at me.

He moves towards the bed and stands between my legs. I have to spread my thighs to give him space, which makes me feel vulnerable, but also alive in a way I've never felt. He runs his fingers over his lips as he studies me, then he lowers his hand and grasps my left tit. Like he's weighing it, he cups my breast, moving up and down before he runs his finger over the sensitive nipple.

I arch my back slightly, pushing my breast further into his hand. His touch is electric, and it feels as if it goes straight to the apex between my thighs. My pussy tingles as my arousal starts to grow.

I close my eyes and suck in a breath, my body tight like an elastic band. When I reopen them he is staring down at me. His eyes never leave mine as he continues to grope me. It feels magnificent. I've never felt anything like this in my life. I've touched myself, I'm only human, but it's not the same as having a stranger's hands on me.

"Why do you need this?" Luke asks again. I can't answer because the truth is so out there no one would ever believe it.

"Kiss me," I say to him softly and brazenly.

He pushes me back onto the bed, the soft mattress cocooning my body as he comes down on top of me. His weight is reassuring in a way I didn't expect. He moves down my body and pushes my dress up to my hips.

Embarrassment floods me at having my underwear exposed to him, but somehow this feels right.

Luke pulls down my underwear. The cooler air from the air con hits my heated pussy, making me gasp. He grabs my hips and slowly leans down, placing a kiss on the most sensitive part of me. I arch my back, an involuntary reaction to what he's doing. He doesn't let up. Luke surprises the hell out of me by licking through my folds up to my clit. The moan that escapes my lips doesn't sound like me. It's wild, and a little bit feral.

His touch ignites a spark inside me, one that burns brightly with every swipe of his tongue. I've never had a man go down on me before, though I have played with and touched myself. It's not the same though. I'm feeling so many emotions it's hard to put into words any of them.

"Luke!" I pant out as his tongue dives into my pussy. I feel self-conscious and awkward, but those feelings are quickly dissipating the more he does to me.

He continues licking, his tongue mystical and magical as it brings me closer and closer to orgasm. He doesn't move from my clit as he inserts something inside me—his finger, I realise. My body wants to push it back out, but he's forceful at keeping it there. After a moment he adds a second finger. Just like when he did this earlier, there is a slight burn at his intrusion, but nothing too painful. I expected sex would hurt. All the girls at school used to complain that it is painful, but so far this has been amazing. All I've felt is pleasure, no pain.

Luke starts to move his fingers, and the way he hooks them inside me makes it feel like he's so deep within me. I feel full in a way I've never felt before.

I can feel pressure building between my legs, my pussy starting to contract as a wave of pleasure builds inside me. I arch my back, pushing him deeper inside me as my orgasm hits. Stars collide behind my eyes and dizziness sweeps through me as my breath tears out of me in heavy pants. I don't know where I am or who I am. I'm just focused on the sensations that are racking my body. The orgasm doesn't last long, and I find myself wanting more—needing more to feel fulfilled.

Luke straightens at the end of the bed and slowly pulls off his shirt. I come up on my elbows to watch him undress, transfixed by the ripples of his body. He is beautiful. All hard lines and sharp edges along with thick muscles.

He undoes his belt and pushes his trousers down, freeing his cock from his boxers. My heart stutters. He's thick and long, and already hard. I'm alarmed by thoughts of how it's supposed to fit inside me, but women do this all the time, and they enjoy it, so I try to relax even as my heart hammers against my ribs.

"Are you sure about this, Alice?" His eyes tell me if I want to stop, he will. That gives me the courage to nod. Better someone of my choosing than a dirty old man who wants to abuse my body because he believes he owns it.

He reaches for his trousers and pulls out his wallet. When he puts it away, he's left holding a foil packet. I watch as he unwraps the condom and rolls it expertly over his cock, making me feel like more of an amateur than I already am. I should know this stuff.

Luke gives his dick two tugs and shakes his head. "I can't believe I'm going to do this."

I hold my breath, thinking he might be about to change his mind. He moves over me and peers down into my eyes but doesn't ask any more questions or make any more excuses. Instead, Luke reaches between our bodies and takes hold of his shaft. Our eyes connect and I feel the warmth spread between us.

Then he pushes inside me.

For a moment I feel pressure and stretching. There is a bite of pain, but it doesn't feel too bad. Relief floods me until I realise he's only got the tip in. He brushes my hair off my face and leans down, kissing me. His lips are soft, gentle even as he claims my mouth. I kiss him back, tasting the alcohol and myself on his tongue as he swipes it inside me. That turns me on more than anything he's done to me tonight. He pulls back slightly. "This is going to hurt."

He pushes his hips against me and his dick slides further inside my channel. I feel a surge of pain as he presses deep inside me. Tears prick my eyes, and I can't stop from crying out as he tears into me. There is so much pressure and burning as I stretch around him. I lie stunned as he kisses along the side of my face and down my neck. "Give it a moment," Luke says. "It will feel better." I believe his promise even though I have no reason to.

He doesn't move. He just keeps still as I get used to his size. I've never felt so full and my thighs open a little more to accommodate him. He is right about the pain: it is starting to subside, and I want him to move. "I'm okay," I tell him.

Luke takes that as his cue to start moving his hips. He rocks his hips back and forth, rolling them as he does. At first the sensation feels weird, but then those tingles start to build again in the depths of my pussy.

I cling to his biceps as he pushes deeper inside me, hitting a spot that makes me gasp each time. The pain melts into pleasure, the tightness I felt becomes looser, and every thrust feels like it's driving me into a new wave of need. He peers into my eyes, and I see the desire in his heavy lids. I've never been looked at like this, like I'm not a prize for him to win. Luke wants to be here, and not because of my name. He doesn't even know my real one, which is something I'm regretting. The urge to hear him say "Sariah" as he slams into me is overwhelming.

"Luke!" I moan as he picks up his rhythm. He circles his hips in a delicious way that makes everything south of my navel stand up and pay attention. Skimming his hand up my belly, he lets it come to rest on my left breast. He squeezes and rubs the nipple, making my pussy quiver.

I can hardly draw breath as he continues to plunge into me. Luke seems like he wants to please me and wants me to enjoy this too. He releases my breast and plays with my clit, rubbing circles over the sensitive bundle of nerves, and I feel like I'm flying out of my body. Everything inside me tenses and I spill over the edge as I push my hips up to meet his. I see stars spilling across my vision as I orgasm harder than I've ever done on my own.

I feel Luke jolt and his hips stutter as he cries out his own release. He moves for a couple of beats inside me before he rubs his hand over my belly gently, in a way that seems at odds with his intimidating nature.

Leaning down, Luke presses a kiss to the side of my mouth before finding my lips. He claims my mouth as if he owns me, and part of me wishes he did. He kisses down my neck before he pulls back, leaning on his palms. He scans my face as if looking for any sign of discomfort. "Okay?"

I nod because my voice has been stolen by what just happened between us. He pulls slowly back, his dick sliding out of me. I feel the loss, and the ache inside me.

He goes into the bathroom and I admire his naked body as he does. He's well built, a Greek Adonis. I didn't know they made men like this.

Luke comes back with a wet towel and presses it between my legs. I flinch and try to push him away, suddenly embarrassed by my nakedness—even though the man has just been inside me.

"What are you doing?" I demand, my voice sounding a little shrill.

"Taking care of you, Alice."

My heart swells at his words. No one has ever taken care of me. Not since my mother died and my father found out the hard truth of her infidelity.

I pull my hands away and let him clean me up. I feel spent, exhausted. I want to sleep for a week, but I don't know the protocol. Will he expect me to leave straight away? Is that what I'm supposed to do?

He tosses the towel into the corner of the room and eyes me. "Did I hurt you?"

"Only for a second," I say, though it's not entirely true. I can still feel his presence between my legs even though he is no longer inside me. I'm sure I'm going to be sore tomorrow, but I can't stop from smiling. I did it. I lost my virginity on my own terms, and when I go to my marital bed with Jeremiah, I'll know my first time was at least pleasant, even if every time after will not be.

Luke climbs onto the bed and pulls me against him. I didn't expect cuddling after so it takes me by surprise. He drags the blanket over us both, covering our naked bodies.

"I've never taken someone's virginity before."

"Tonight was a night of many firsts," I say.

"Do you want to tell me why you were so insistent on losing your virginity to a stranger?"

I shake my head. "Does it matter? We both got something out of it." I peer up his chest to his face, my stomach suddenly churning. "Was I bad?"

The look on Luke's face is a picture. His brows draw down as he takes in my words. "No, little dove, you were not bad." He kisses my temple in an oddly tender way.

We lie clinched together for what feels like hours. I doze against his chest, loving the feel of having someone wrapped around me. As I come around it takes me a second to realise where I am, and panic clutches my stomach. I've been here too long and I need to get home. Luke is asleep with his head turned to the side and his sandy-blond hair dripping over his closed eyes.

I extract myself carefully from his grip and pull the covers back to climb out of the bed. As I sit up, he grabs my wrist.

"Where are you going?"

I spin around, aware of how naked I am, and pull the covers against my chest. He seems amused by my gesture, and why wouldn't he be? The horse has already left the stable. He has seen more of my body than anybody ever has in my life. "I need to get home."

His eyes narrow. "Why?"

"I've already been gone too long." I don't want to risk Declan finding me gone.

He takes this out of context. Anger clouds his face. "You got someone waiting for you at home?"

His words surprise me. "Do you think I would sleep with you if did?" There's a hint of anger in my words, and for good reason. I am many things, but I'm not a cheat. No one owns me yet.

I have no idea how to undo the deal my father's made, but there must be a way. I do not want to be Mrs Sariah Wood. The thought makes my skin crawl as if I am covered in bugs.

"I don't know," he says. "I don't know the first thing about you."

Some of my anger fades because he's right; he doesn't know anything about me.

Just as I don't know anything about him.

And that is how it has to stay.

"I have to go," I repeat.

He releases his hold on my wrist and I move to find my clothes so I can redress. "Meet me again."

I twist around to look at him, surprised by his words. "Why?"

His brows come together once more, and I get the impression I've confused him. "Because one time wasn't enough."

I should say no, but part of me wants to see him again. I chew on my bottom lip for a moment. "I can't promise anything."

I can't.

Getting out of the house once was risky enough. Doing it again is playing with fire. If my father catches me, he'll beat me bloody.

"I come to the club most Fridays," he says. "Be there next week."

I nod, elation washing through me that he wants to see me again.

Once I'm dressed, I grab my clutch bag and head for the door. I pause before stepping through it and twist back to him. "You have no idea what you did for me tonight. Thank you."

Before he can say anything else, I slip out of the room and rush down the corridor to make my way home. But my head is full of Luke and the hope that perhaps we could be more than we are.

CHAPTER 6

Lucas

"**A**re you fucking listening?" Kane demands. I snap my gaze towards my brother, realising I haven't heard a word he's said.

I'm thinking about Alice. The way she felt beneath me is etched into my brain. That wide-eyed innocence is impossible to encounter among the women I normally sleep with. I find it damn enticing.

But Alice isn't who she says she is.

There are secrets in her eyes, and lies. I shouldn't get embroiled. Fuck knows I have enough shit to deal with, but I can't stop thinking about her and her predicament, whatever that may be.

"Well, you were being boring," I mutter, earning a glare from a man who can kill me with his bare hands. I don't fear my brother.

"Your head has been stuck up your arse all day," he grumbles. "The fuck is wrong with you?"

"Nothing is wrong with me." I shift my gaze to the floor-to-ceiling window of the office we are sitting in, overlooking the London skyline. Fraser Holdings has business interests across the globe, both legal and illegal. The latter fly under the radar, hidden from view, but they make as much money as the above board shit. It's the only reason we continue to do it.

That and because my father likes the power.

As does my mother.

She would never allow Anthony to give this life up. And we all know Anthony Fraser does whatever Charlotte tells him.

"Yet you're barely focused. Do you even know what I told you?"

Since I have no idea, I shake my head. He's right. I am unfocused and I need to not be. All I can think about is whether my little dove will be waiting in the bar for me.

"Was it interesting?" I'm being a dick and I know it. If I was anyone else, Kane would have put his fist through my fucking face, but despite his temper my brother has never laid a hand on any of his siblings.

"I was talking about our mother and how she's moving pieces on the board. Again."

I let out a breath and shift my shoulders. "When isn't Charlotte moving shit on the board?"

Kane can't argue with that, and he doesn't try to. Our mother is a meddlesome bitch. She plays Anthony like a fiddle, making him dance to whatever tune she wishes. Anthony might think he's the head of the family, but he's wrong. Power has never been his but Charlotte's.

"She's trying to cement an alliance with the Adams's."

I snap my eyes towards him. The Adams's are another crime syndicate who operate in London. Like us they own a slice of territory, a small piece of a larger pie, but they are powerful. They have contacts and the ability to cause chaos if they choose, so keeping them onside is always a good idea.

For the first time in a long time, the syndicates of London are all at peace. War is a dangerous and expensive undertaking. We all try to avoid it as much as possible, and we have been successful for a while. We currently have a tenuous peace with the other firms, so I'm not sure why my mother wants to shore it up even more. What would we have to gain from an alliance that is already in place? "Why?"

"She fears the Eastons. They are gaining strength and becoming more powerful in their own right. She wants to ensure we have the means to stand against them should they decide to come at us."

I have met Declan Easton a few times over the years. He is a first-class arsehole, but he's not a stupid man. He doesn't strike me as someone who would come after his allies just to gain more power.

"Why does she fear them?"

Kane pushes up from his seat and goes to the window, digging his hands into the pockets of his suit trousers. The view is spectacular, and it looks down over Canary Wharf. He's used to it, as I am, but I still can't stop myself from staring at the tiny twinkling lights starting to appear on the dusk skyline.

"There is a rumour that Declan means to marry his daughter to Jeremiah Wood."

Wood has territory in Manchester, a city north of London. It has a reputation for gun crime, drugs, and all manner of nefarious acts that rival those of the capital. In fact, a few years back it was known as Gunchester because of the amount of gun crime. Lately Manchester has been exerting power, seeing itself as a key player in the criminal underbelly of England. It's something I told my father time and time again we need to quash. Those fuckers believing they are on our level is dangerous.

Knowing Wood is trying to build alliances within the capital is fucking cause for concern. What the hell is he hoping to achieve? And why does Easton want to marry his daughter to a man like that? Wood is known as 'the Butcher.' He has a dark reputation that mirrors our own. Ruthless, cold, and calculating, he's not a man to trifle with.

"Who is the daughter?" I ask. I don't recall her. In truth she's not on my radar. She is not someone I need to worry about.

"Charlotte says her name is Sariah. I've never seen her—not in public. From what I hear, Declan keeps her locked up tight and has done since she was a little girl."

That's not unusual. We keep Aurelia out of the limelight too. Fear that she may be used against us, kidnapped, or hurt is always in the back of our minds. So we don't draw attention to our sister in the hopes people will forget she exists.

At least until she's ready to marry.

I have no doubt my mother has planned an alliance for our sister that will secure our position further. Kane will also have his wife chosen for him, as Zeke should have. He'd broken every rule by choosing his own. Though I suspect my parents were not too upset with his choice of wife. Bailey brings the alliance of the Untamed Sons Motorcycle Club.

"So how does Charlotte plan on cementing an alliance with the Adams's?" I ask, although I have a good idea. Alliances are either gained through marriage or deals. I do know Hamish Adams has a couple of daughters, though I don't remember their names.

Kane's mouth pulls into a tight line and his eyes darken for a moment. "She wants me to marry the eldest daughter."

I run my fingers over the top of the table, my gaze going to the window once more. "And what do you think about that?"

"I have no desire to wed the Adams bitch."

I figured that would be his response. He has known his whole life that he will marry out of obligation rather than choice, but there is a difference between knowing and having the option presented in front of you.

"We must all do what we do not want to," I mutter, even though I share Kane's dismay at the idea. Sometimes, I wonder what it would be like to not play games, to live a simple, normal life, to not be considered a pawn in a game that can never be won.

It's a stupid thought. Our lives were planned out for us from the moment we drew our first breath. Just as my brothers and my sister will be pushed into a marriage of our parents' choosing, so will I. There are no choices when you are a Fraser. I don't believe Charlotte or Anthony would try to kill us if we didn't obey them, but if we broke away from the Fraser Firm we would be hunted by the other families. There is no normal life for us. There is only blood and death. This is our cross to bear and we carry the load, because the alternative is being annihilated by our enemies.

"Indeed," Kane sneers. My eldest brother is not happy about this arrangement, but I know he will do what is expected.

"Have you seen the girl?" I ask. Not that it matters if she's ugly as sin. If Charlotte has decided this is a match that will be made, it will go ahead.

"A photograph. She is not a troll. Actually she's quite pretty. I just don't want her as my fucking wife."

There's nothing I can say to my brother to ease this path for him, so I hold my tongue. Any words would be empty anyway.

An alliance with the Adams's would be beneficial and would shore up defences against any form of Easton growth. It still doesn't make it any easier to bear.

"Our time will come for each of us," I say softly. I dread the day my mother and father pick my bride. "It would be good to have the Adams syndicate on board. A marriage will ensure those bonds."

Kane makes a grunting sound deep in his throat and turns

away. "Don't worry, little brother, I know how to do my duty. I will marry the Adams bitch because it will help secure our position. Am I happy about it? No, but I will do what is expected."

The sacrifices we make....

"It won't be as bad as you think." The words are empty. It will be worse.

"It is easy for you to say this when it's not you who is facing a lifetime of marriage with someone you haven't chosen."

"I'm not going to choose either," I remind him.

Kane drags his fingers through his hair, his frustration etched onto every inch of his face. We are no longer young boys but men with a kingdom spread beneath our feet.

"Just be aware mother is plotting," Kane warns me. "You might find yourself in the firing line next."

I shudder at the thought. I'm considerably younger than Kane. There are two years between Kane and Zeke and three years between me and Zeke. Aurelia is four years younger than me and just turned eighteen a month ago.

I know my time is coming, that the clock is ticking down, but I hold onto the thought that I might have a little bit of freedom still.

"Maybe we should do as Zeke did. Make our own alliances," I mutter.

Kane shakes his head. "I have no interest in marriage."

This doesn't surprise me, considering how tumultuous our parents' marriage has been. I push up from the desk wrapping my knuckles against the wood. "Keep me informed," I tell him.

I've had enough of the conversation. I don't want to think about my impending future.

It's Friday night.

A week since I last saw Alice.

I said I would meet her again. I have no idea if she will show, but I have to go and see. Part of me hopes she will be there, because I'm not done with her yet.

Kane doesn't rise as I leave the room, too stuck inside his own head. I make my way down the corridor towards the exit. I'm so deep in thought I don't notice Talia, my father's assistant, coming out of the kitchen. We collide and I reach out to steady her as she totters back on her high-heeled shoes. Her manicured nails scrape over my arms as she holds on to me. Her flaming red hair is curled today, though the woman seems like she has a different style every day. "Mr Fraser... I'm so sorry. I wasn't paying attention—"

I cut her off before she can continue. "It's fine," I say and release my hold on her. "Shouldn't you have gone home by now? It's late."

She gives me a wry smile. "Mr Fraser needs me to help him draft some proposals."

My father is a fucking dick. It's late. Talia should be home.

She has been with my father for as long as I can remember. Her father is one of our lieutenants, a man called Parker Weston. He is loyal as fuck, and my father trusts his daughter with his most intimate secrets. She has proven herself over the years, yet she is still wary of us. That fear is inbuilt in the Fraser name.

"Make sure someone from security walks you to your car."
"I will."

I continue to the lift and push the button to call it to the floor. When I get down to the foyer, Winters is waiting for me. He leads me out to my car and together we climb in. I let him drive as my brain is fucking tired after the day I've had. I should have got Alice's number. I want to be able to contact her whenever I want to. This uncertainty about whether she'll show or not has me on fucking edge, but as much as it pisses me off, it also thrills me. I enjoy the chase.

Winters drives me home and I get showered and changed before heading back out to Tease. As always I bypass the line and head straight for the door. The bouncer lets me through and I step into the club. It's not as busy as it was last week, but then it is earlier. I didn't want to risk her coming before I was here.

I go over to the bar, ignoring the thumping of the music. The bartender instantly starts to make my drink. I turn back into the room and peer through the flashing lights. I don't see my blonde-haired beauty anywhere.

For the next hour I sit at the bar, waiting like a loser. I'm debating leaving when I catch a glimpse of golden hair from across the room.

Alice.

She spots me and her eyes dart around before she slowly walks towards me, pushing through the crowd of people that has swelled since I've been sitting here. I take a moment to drink her in, loving the way she looks. As she was last time, she is wearing a summer dress that makes her look completely out of place amongst the other women. It reaches just above her knees, exposing her legs.

I can't stop the grin from creeping across my face as she approaches. She peers up at me through dark lashes and I can tell by the look on her face she is not sure what she's doing here.

"Hello, Alice."

CHAPTER 7

Sariah

I have no idea what I'm doing here. This is playing with fire. Getting out of the house once was a miracle on its own, but doing it again is reckless. If my father finds out what I'm doing, he will beat me bloody. There will be no talking my way out of it. He will never understand my need for freedom, even if it is an illusion.

As I step through the doors of Tease, my heart starts to race. This is a mistake. I'm not even sure that I believe Luke will be here, despite his assurances he wanted me to meet him again. In my experience people make promises they don't keep, and I don't expect Luke will be any different.

He had been gentle when he had taken me to bed, which was more than I'd anticipated from a man who looks like him. My first time had been nothing like what I expected, but I don't have any regrets. He had taken care of me as best he could, and I can never thank him enough for that. I know Jeremiah would not have afforded me the same privilege or courtesy.

I'm glad he wanted to see me. The thought of never seeing Luke again made my belly swirl unpleasantly. He left his mark on me, and not just from the way I could feel him inside me for days after he fucked me, but because he was the first man who treated me like a human being and not a bartering chip.

There is something heady about that—something that makes me feel alive. Like there's something worth fighting for.

As the crowd parts, I see him standing near the bar. There's no denying Luke is a handsome man. I know he's dangerous though. I've been around men like him my entire life. My father is one of them.

In this moment Declan Easton is the last thing on my mind. All I'm focused on is the handsome man in front of me. He hasn't yet noticed me weaving through the crowd. I could disappear, leave as if I was never here, but my feet keep pushing forward. I don't understand how to explain it, and I don't want to, either. For the first time in my life, I'm doing something for me, and that feels good.

His eyes suddenly lock onto mine and I feel drenched in heat as his gaze roams over me. I know I'm dressed differently from the girls here. I don't have the tight miniskirts and the barely-there tops that reveal far too much midriff. I look like a Sunday school teacher, because this outfit is the type of thing my father's assistant buys for me. I'm not allowed to get my own wardrobe. It's just one of the many ways in which I'm controlled.

As I move closer to Luke, my legs start to feel jellied. This is a bad idea, but my heart screams at me to keep going. I'm about to be pushed into a lifetime of servitude to a man I don't love. I want something that's mine, even if it's only for a short time.

I stop in front of him, and he dips his head without warning, claiming my mouth. I freeze, shocked at his audacity, and then I melt against him. His mouth feels good against mine, and as he slips his tongue inside, I can't stop from meeting it.

His fingers press against my back, pulling me closer, and I allow it because I want it too.

I didn't know it could be like this or feel like this. He makes my stomach flip in a way it's never done before. Luke makes me want things I can't have, like the ability to choose my own partner.

My legs feel weak as he continues to take my mouth. I don't want this moment to end, but it has to. I wish I could say clinched with him, wrapped up in him, but in a few weeks' time my life will change for the worse.

And there's nothing I can do about it.

He pulls back, a little breathless, and skims his knuckles down my cheek. "I wasn't sure you were going to show."

He has no idea how close I came to staying away.

"I wasn't sure I was coming either," I admit.

He rubs his fingers over my arms, his touch eliciting a blast of heat through me. I can't help but to lean into his touch. I feel safe in a way I never have.

"I'm glad you did." He takes my hand and leads me into the VIP area. Memories assault me as we walk through the corridor where he pinned me against the wall and claimed my mouth for the first time.

Heat rises in my cheeks as I think about where his hands had gone and about how much I liked it.

He pulls me into the bar area. It's different back here to the main floor. Everything is plush and velvet, the dark-purple painted walls offset with gold finishings. I let him guide me into a booth where I sit next to him. His hand instantly goes to my thigh and his touch is reassuring as he signals a waitress over.

"Scotch for me," Luke says in his dark gravelly voice that goes straight to the apex between my thighs. "What will you have?"

"Oh, um, I'll just have a glass of wine."

It feels like a safe order, but I don't know what else I would like. My father doesn't let me drink at home, and it's not like I'm out to galas every night.

Luke rubs my thigh and I pulse with need between my legs. I wish he would stroke just a little bit higher to that sensitive bundle of nerves that needs attention. I urge him mentally to do it, but he doesn't.

Neither of us speaks until the waitress returns with our drinks. As soon as the wine glass is placed in front of me, I take a long sip, needing the courage of the alcohol. I shouldn't feel nervous. This man has been inside me, has seen my most intimate parts, but I do. I feel the need to please him.

He cups my face, bringing my attention to his eyes, which are pinning me. "I'm glad you came."

I am too, despite the risk. I don't expect him to want to make small talk, but that's precisely what he does.

"Tell me about yourself, Alice."

I didn't expect that and I'm wary. How can I tell him anything without revealing who I really am?

"There's nothing to tell," I reply dismissively. "I'm really rather boring."

"You're many things. Boring is not one of them." His fingers trail over my skin, making me feel hot between my legs. A few inches north and he would be touching me. I need it. Want it.

"You barely know me."

"That can change. Do you have brothers? Sisters?"

"Neither. What about you?"

"I have two brothers and a sister." He takes a sip of his drink.

"Are you close?" I'm unable to keep the curiosity out of my voice.

"Yes. I don't think my parents ever intended to make us as close as we are."

"Why do you say that?"

He leans into me, and I get a noseful of his masculine scent. "Because we're a united force against them." His smile is dark, but I find my own lips curving up at the corners.

"Are you the eldest?"

"The second youngest, actually. My sister is the baby of the family."

I always wanted a brother, someone who would stand between me and Declan. I never had that buffer.

"You protect her?"

"With my life." The response is not empty. I can tell by the fierceness in his eyes. "My sister and my brothers are everything to me. I would die to defend any one of them."

Jealousy rears its ugly head. No one has ever done that for me.

As we talk, I feel myself growing closer to him, wanting to know everything about him. It's a foolish want, but in the moment I allow myself to hope.

And that is dangerous.

Hope makes a person want things that can't be theirs, and it pushes them into impossible situations. Luke and I can never be more than what we are now, and that hurts. The first time in my life that I feel like I've found someone I could share my time with, someone I feel comfortable with, and I can't have him.

"What do you do for a living?" I ask.

He seems to find this amusing, because his lips quirk into a smirk. "A little of this and a little of that. My family owns a few businesses around the city."

I cock my brow, impressed by this. "You're a businessman?"

"I'm a man who gets what he wants," Luke says in a voice that makes my stomach quiver. He has a way of making me feel like the most important thing in the room.

"And what is it you want?"

He leans into me, his nose skimming up the column of my throat. "You, little dove." Butterflies take flight inside my belly. "What do you say we get out of here?"

"And go where?" I ask, holding my breath. I would like a repeat performance of the last time we were together, but I'm not sure if that's what he wants.

"A hotel." He kisses along the line of my jaw, and I feel my body turn to jelly with each press of his lips. I want to go with him, desperately. I'm not thinking rationally. I'm just acting on what I want. "Okay."

He tips his glass and drains it of scotch before grabbing my hand and pulling out of the booth. As we step out of it, I notice a man waiting at the side. It's the same man who had driven us to the hotel. "Who's the man who follows you?"

I've seen enough bodyguards to know this man is Luke's. Why would Luke need a bodyguard?

"His name is Winters. Just ignore him. I do."

I trail behind Luke, my feet struggling to keep up with him and his long legs. "Is he your bodyguard?"

He stops in his tracks and turns to look back at me. "And what would a pretty girl in a sundress know of bodyguards?"

Have I given too much away? The suspicion in his eyes makes my heart thump a beat. "I was just joking." The lie falls easily from my tongue. I feel like my whole life has become one big fabrication. I'm lying to Luke about who I really am, and I'm lying to my father about staying in the house.

He relaxes a little and rubs his thumb over the back of my hand which is still clutched in his. "He's here to protect me."

Now it's me who's feeling suspicious. "A businessman needs protection?"

He doesn't miss a beat when he says, "When your family is worth as much as mine, the answer is yes."

That makes sense and it goes some way to soothing me.

It's not like I think Luke is not genuine. Or that it matters. He is just something to pass the time until I am taken to my doom.

"Telling me you have money might be a dangerous move. What if I'm a gold digger?" I lift my lips at the corners, contradicting my words with humour.

"Are you?"

"I've found that money doesn't buy happiness," I say, and it's not a lie. I have money, or rather my father has money, and I've never been happy a day in my life from the moment my mother died.

"Now that we can both agree on."

He leads me out into the cold air, and I shiver a little against the chill as it caresses my skin. Winters heads over to talk to the valet while Luke pulls me against his side to keep me warm.

"You didn't think to bring a coat?" He shrugs out of his jacket and wraps it around my shoulders. It's an oddly intimate gesture that both confuses and warms me.

The women in the queue are wearing next to nothing and must be freezing. They don't seem to care though. I get the impression fashion takes precedence over being warm for these girls. My reason for not wearing a coat is because my jackets are kept in the mud room downstairs, and it was too risky to claim one.

"No one else here is wearing one."

Luke continues to stroke the back of my hand as we wait for the car to be brought around.

Winters steps forward as the car comes to a stop. He opens the back door and Luke and I slip inside. It's warmer within the car, though not by much.

"Are you still cold?" Luke asks.

I nod. It takes effort to stop my teeth from chattering. Luke leans forward as Winters climbs into the front seat, and he orders him to put the heating on. When he sits back, he pulls me against him, rubbing his hands up my arms.

Tired, I lean my head against his shoulder, but I'm thrilled at the prospect of being with him again. When I'm with him I feel like a different person, like I could escape from my destiny. I forget about the storm that is coming for me. I am just Sariah.

Or Alice.

There is something freeing about being somebody else, even if it means that everything between Luke and me is based on a lie. I feel those shackles around my wrists loosen a little bit, giving me room to breathe, room to be myself, though in truth I have no idea who Sariah is. I've always been whoever my father decreed I should be. His pretty little marionette that dances to whatever tune he plays.

I'm done dancing. I want my life to be my own. I don't know where things between me and Luke are going, but I want to build on it, explore it further if I choose. I want to be in charge of my own fate.

But it's a dream.

I am my father's little bird, caught in a gilded cage. If I defy him, he will tell the world I am not his. I don't know what kind of threats I would face because of that, but I know it would not be good to find out.

People like me get swallowed whole by the monster that is the criminal underbelly of London. I wouldn't stand a chance out there on my own, and my father—Declan—tells me that often.

I need to stop referring to him as my father. He has shown he does not care for me as a parent should, so I should not afford him the title. He does not deserve it.

I've thought many times about trying to find my father, my real one, but I have no idea where to start. My mother kept that secret and took it to the grave with her. I doubt

Declan knows either, because he would have started a war if he had.

"Are you okay?" Luke asks. "You disappeared into yourself there."

I give him a smile, chasing my demons away and putting them back in the boxes I have created over the years to protect myself. "I'm fine," I assure him.

He doesn't seem convinced, but he doesn't push either, which I appreciate. Getting into my messy life is not something I want to do with a stranger.

And as much as I enjoy Luke's company, that's exactly what he is. I don't know the true face of the man who is taking me to another hotel room to fuck me. All I know is what I see and that should be enough to scare me, but it's not.

Neither of us speaks as the car pulls up outside the hotel. I peer up at the building, taking in the old architecture and the rounded window tops. The redbrick makes it look elegant and of a different time.

I let Luke lead me into the building, barely focused as he checks us in. Winters follows us, as always Luke's shadow.

My mind is racing. I shouldn't be doing this again. I already played with fire once. My father has spies everywhere. If I am seen, it would be a death sentence for me, and for Luke too probably. I study the side of his face, hating myself for putting him in this position. He is innocent, and he doesn't deserve the hellfire that will rain down if we're found out. My guilt gnaws at me, a cancer that needs to be rooted out. It poisons my blood.

Armed with a key card, we make our way to the lift. Luke stabs the button to call it down, not letting go of my hand the whole time. I feel reassured by his touch.

The doors slide shut, and as soon as they do, Luke is on me. He pushes me against the wall of the lift and takes my mouth in a bruising claim. He kisses me with a desperate passion that makes my toes curl in my shoes. I feel like I'm flying, like my body is lifted off the ground, even though it's not. Every touch, every swipe of his mouth over mine, is pure ecstasy, a dream.

One I intend to make the most of.

I skim my fingers up the back of his shirt, feeling the skin beneath. It's warm, like silk, and I can't stop from rubbing over him like a cat marking its territory. As his lips press against my neck, I can't stop the whimper that erupts from my mouth. My whole body feels electrified as he touches me with whisper softness.

"I'm going to fuck you, little dove. Would you like that?"

My body screams yes! I want to feel him on top of me again. I want to be surrounded by him. He is sunshine in a cloudy sky, even though I can see the grey storm clouds rolling in. "Yes," I gasp as he hits a particularly sensitive spot on my neck.

He skims his hand down my body and cups me between my legs. He must be able to feel the heat and the wetness there. My underwear is soaked from the anticipation that has built inside me. My body remembers the delicious soreness after he had taken me the first time, and it wants a repeat performance.

"Luke...." His name comes out on a rush of air that I can hardly control. I want to taste him, so I try to kiss up the side of his face, but I can hardly concentrate as he dips his finger inside my underwear and pushes it into me.

My eyes fly open. Winters is standing just feet from where we are, although he's facing forward, giving the illusion of privacy by keeping his back to us. It is one thing to be kissing Luke; it is another to have his fingers in my pussy. I try to push his hands away, but he won't allow it. As he hits the spot that makes my legs shake, I don't even care if we have an audience. The groan that rips from my mouth is primal and uncontrollable.

"That's it, Alice. That's what I want. You begging me for more."

His voice and his words nearly push me over the edge. How is it possible for a man to sound so delectable with just a few sentences?

Winters doesn't say a word as he gets out of the lift and starts walking towards the room. Luke straightens my dress and takes my hand again. I like that he always wants to be touching me. It makes me feel wanted, desired, needed.

We stop in front of the door, and Winters opens it with the key card. He steps into the room first, and I start to follow, but Luke pulls me back with a slight shake of his head. "Let Winters do his checks."

We wait for him to finish checking the bathroom and the rest of the room. When he's done, he comes back to the door and gives Luke a nod.

Luke lets Winters out of the room, shutting the door behind him. I glance briefly around before Luke is on me. He pushes me against the wall nearest to the door and grinds against me. My pussy quivers as he does it and I can't help from pressing back. He attacks my mouth with fervour, claiming me and taking what he wants.

He shoves my dress up and dips his fingers into my underwear once again, finishing what he started in the lift. I circle my hips, trying to push him deeper inside me. He pistons his fingers quickly in and out, making my breath catch in my throat. I want more. I need it. I didn't realise how much until this moment.

I go over the edge, moaning his name, my pussy pulsing and contracting around his fingers. It makes me dizzy, my breath lodging in my throat as I try to draw air in.

Withdrawing his hand from inside my underwear, Luke

lifts me, and I instinctively wrap my legs around his hips. He walks us both to the bed, his mouth locked on mine as we go. I want him to fulfil his promise and fuck me. There's an achy feeling between my legs that only he can soothe.

He lays me on the mattress and comes down on top of me even as he undoes his trousers. His eyes meet mine for a moment, and like before, heat passes between us. He kisses me before he rolls on a condom. I wait, feeling exposed as his heated eyes focus on me. Then he slides into me, making every thought in my head shatter.

CHAPTER 8
Lucas

I wake expecting to find her draped over me, but Alice has gone. The side of the bed where she was lying is cold to the touch, and there's no sign of her clothes on the floor where we had discarded them last night. I get out of the bed and go to the bathroom. I switch on the light, but the bathroom is empty too.

I grab the white towel robe off the back of the door and slip into it before pulling the door of the room open. Winters is leaning against the wall next to it, and he peers at me as I step out into the corridor. "Alice?" I ask him.

"She left about an hour ago."

Fuck.

I wanted to get her number, so I can talk to her between our meetups—if she even comes to another one. This thing may have run its course, but I'm not ready for it to end. I still want to explore more with her. She interests me. I need to find out every intimate detail about her and who she is. I don't like mysteries, and she sure as fuck is one. My thoughts are consumed by her more than I would like. I'm not a man who is given to emotions—usually.

"And you just let her go?" I snap. Fucking useless bastard.

"I wasn't aware I was meant to keep her here."

He makes a good point. I never told him that he had to. I didn't expect Alice would run. She's like a skittish fawn, and I want to know why. What has made her this way? And how can I fix it?

I go back into the room and shut the door behind me. I notice something sparkling in the light from the bedside table. As I get closer, I see a gold bracelet on the bedside table. It's pretty, inlaid with diamonds, and it looks expensive, not to mention old. She must have left it when she ran out. I pocket it.

A trophy of our tryst.

I hate not being in control, but all I can do is hope she shows at the club again and that she's as interested in me as I am in her.

TWO NIGHTS LATER I'M AT ONE OF OUR UNDERGROUND fights. I haven't seen Alice since that night, and she hasn't been to Tease in that time—or so the bar staff have reported to me. Her sudden departure from the hotel room before I was finished with her irritated me. That anger has been gnawing at my gut since. Women don't walk out on me.

Ever.

That she did has me feeling mixed things—rage but also a modicum of respect that she isn't someone who just does as I command.

I'm hoping the fight will scratch some of that frustration I'm feeling. I need the violence, crave it even, but tonight is different. I need an outlet for what I'm feeling.

The fight helps me to release some of the tension rolling through me.

I oversee more of these now that my brother is happily married. I don't mind. In fact, I quite like the scene. The mindless violence makes my blood roar. There's something gratifying about watching a grown man beat the shit out of a weaker opponent. Plus, we make a lot of money doing this.

Tonight is an unusual night. The Untamed Sons Motorcycle Club is here in full force. One of the brothers, a guy known as Cage, is fighting in about an hour. I'm not on edge, but shit has a habit of getting rowdy around these fuckers.

I spot their president, Ravage, talking with Nox, his vice president. The guy is fucking huge, though I don't fear him.

He raises eyes and catches mine. I can tell he is debating not coming over, but he does eventually extract himself from his brothers and make his way over. Nox follows on his heels, and he gives me a frosty look as he gets closer. He endures Zeke because he has no choice. Since Zeke is married to his sister, Bailey, he is family, whether Nox wants it that way or not. Considering what my brother did, he is lucky he is still breathing. He might be married to Bailey now, and things may be settled, but that wasn't always the case. He stole her after he was meant to rescue her. I'm not sure the Sons have ever forgiven us for that.

Winters moves closer to my back as Ravage and Nox approach. I don't need his protection. I can take care of myself. I'd shoot him a scowl, but I don't want to look weak in front of these men.

"I'd say it's good to see you," I say mildly, "but I don't think you'd agree."

"What makes you think that? The Frasers are friends to the Sons," Ravage says, giving me a tight-lipped smile.

Yeah, he doesn't really see it that way either.

My brother humiliated his club, but it was better to make an alliance than it was to go to war. There would have been unnecessary deaths and wars cost money. Neither side wanted that, especially us.

Ravage glances behind him towards the ring. There are

two competitors going at it inside the cage. The cheers are loud as one of the men gets the other on the ground with his legs wrapped around his neck. Both have blood streaming from their heads, which is not an unusual sight during these fights.

"Heard there could be a wedding on the horizon. Declan Easton is marrying his daughter to Jeremiah Wood."

This catches me a little off guard. I keep my expression unreadable. I'm surprised Ravage is aware of what is going on in the syndicates, though I shouldn't be. I'm sure the Sons keep their finger on the pulse of everything happening in London, just as we do.

"So I've heard."

"It doesn't worry you?" Nox asks.

I give him my attention. "Should it?"

"Easton is bringing together London and Manchester. He is creating a powerhouse. Yeah, that fucking worries me."

He's not wrong. It's the same fear that upset my mother, and it's the reason why she's pushing Kane to marry into the Adams syndicate. Charlotte no doubt hopes that will create a secure alliance. Maybe I should be worried, but the only thing on my mind is Alice and finding her. I don't want to let this woman slip through my fingers, and relying on her coming back on Friday seems risky. The politics of the city don't interest me right now.

"When you're top of the food chain, you'll find there is nothing that really worries you." I straighten my suit jacket, my words strong. I don't want the Sons to see even the hint of a chink in my armour.

Nox growls at me under his breath. I can't stop smirking at the fact that I've pissed him off. Annoying these bastards is the only thing that keeps me fucking sane. I live to torment.

"You're not as close to the top of that tree as you think you are," Ravage says with a sneer.

Touched a nerve. It makes my smirk grow even as I feel Winters move closer to my back, sensing trouble might be brewing.

I get up in Ravage's face, ignoring how Nox tries to move between us. I'm sure his other brothers are preparing to make a move, and the air becomes still, fraught with tension. Any sane person would back down. "Why don't you let the big boys worry about who is marrying who. You children just play with your bikes."

Ravage wraps his hands around my throat. It's a ballsy move, and I have to respect him for his show of strength. "You're family now, which is the only reason I'm not putting my fist into your fucking face. But don't cross me, Lucas. You won't like the wrath of the Sons."

Is that supposed to scare me? It doesn't. He might have the weight of an MC behind him, but I'm hardly defenceless.

"And you think you would like the might of the Fraser syndicate coming down on your head?"

The tension continues to swell. It's Nox who breaks the silence. "This marriage is a concern for us, and it should be for you. You decide you want to pull your head out of your arse long enough to talk about it, I will arrange a meet."

I watch the two of them walk off and rejoin their brothers. I don't give a fuck about this wedding. I don't understand why everyone cares either. So Wood marries the Easton bitch. What fucking difference does that make? Wood is an insignificant drug baron. He is hardly powerful enough to take down the rest of us, and Easton is a cunt with no fucking idea what he's doing. It's partly why he's marrying his daughter to a man with little to no sway.

I watch the fights for a little while before I head back to the staff area and the office. Winters keeps guard outside the room like the good little dog he is. I sit at the desk with my feet on top of the wood, trying to clear my head. We are not enemies of the Eastons, but we're not exactly allies either. They stay to their corners and we stay in ours, and that's how it's always been. No one wants to interfere in another syndicate's business. It's a sure-fire way to cause a shitstorm.

I drum my fingers on the table as I mull over what the Sons said. Maybe Charlotte is right to ensure our own chain has no weak links.

Though I doubt Kane would agree.

I should dial my mother or my father and tell them what transpired. Instead, I find myself calling Eric Granger. He's our go-to guy whenever we need techie stuff.

He answers on the third ring, and I don't bother with any preamble. "I need you to find someone for me."

"Give me everything you know about them, and I'll see what I can do."

Granger has access to places that most people would never be able to stomach going to. It makes him a good person to know.

I tell him everything I can remember about Alice, including the fact that I'm sure she's using a fake name. Granger doesn't say a word as I talk, waiting until I'm finished to say, "It's not a lot to go on, but I'll see what I can find."

I hang up and tap my fingers against the desk again. I feel restless. I wish she were here, but for now, I have to rely on the memory of her. She doesn't know it yet, but when I find her, I plan on keeping her. No more games. No more sneaking around. I'm going to own her heart, body, and soul.

Sariah

I make my way to the club on Monday night. It's not the Friday, as we normally plan, but my need to see him is overwhelming. I don't think I can last another few days. I have no idea if he'll be there, but I hope he will. Getting out of the house is becoming harder. The closer I get to the wedding, the more the hold my father has on me heightens. I know he's worried something might happen to me before I have a chance to say my vows.

If only.

I queue outside for what feels like forever, shivering against the cold, before I am finally granted access to the club. Tease is busy. Sweaty bodies are pressed together, swaying in time to the music that thumps through the floor. I scan the room, searching for his blond hair, but I don't see him anywhere.

I make my way over to the bar, and the man behind it gives me a dimpled smile. He moves away, grabbing his phone from the back shelf of the bar and texting something before coming back to me. "What can I get you?"

I order a glass of wine and move towards the end of the bar, leaning against the wood as I keep scanning the space. It was a longshot to imagine Luke would just be hanging out here all the time, but I had hoped. I'll finish my wine, and then I'll leave if he is not here by then.

When I finish my drink, I slide the empty glass back onto the bar and start to push away, but the bartender shakes his head. "You wait. He's on his way."

I narrow my eyes at him. "How do you know that?"

"Because I let him know you were here. He told me to message him if you turned up." He pushes another glass of wine in front of me, and when I reach into my purse to pay him, he shakes his head. "He's opened a bar tab for you."

The way Luke takes care of me even when he's not here makes me feel loved in a way I've not felt in years. It makes me feel wanted, desired, beautiful. As if I'm worthy of someone's attention. I didn't know that was possible.

After what feels like forever, I see him moving through the crowd. His blond head towers over most of the crowd, and his eyes find mine as soon as he gets close. He locks his gaze to mine, and a smile forms on his face. My heart skips a beat. He's just as handsome as I remember—more so in fact. Every time I see him, I fall for him a little more. If I'm being honest, I'm already besotted with the man who showed me attention.

"Little dove."

He trails his fingers down my cheek, stroking me softly as he does. The heat in his eyes dampens down the darkness and is less threatening. I have no doubt he is still dangerous, but not towards me.

"I wasn't sure if I made a mistake by coming."

He brushes his lips over mine, and I can't stop from melting against him. I could easily give my heart to this man, let down my walls, and I wish that could be our future together. I wish I could have him and he me.

"I'm glad you're here."

As am I. We are surrounded by people, some dancing, some waiting to get drinks at the bar, so when Luke slips his hand under my dress, I stiffen. My eyes dart around as I grab his wrist, stopping his exploration of my pussy. I'm wet. I have been from the moment he walked up to me. He makes my body react in ways I didn't know it could. He makes me feel alive, like my skin is flaming with heat.

He continues to kiss me, ignoring my protest as his finger slides under my underwear and through my folds. I shouldn't do it, but I widen my stance a little, giving him better access to my most private part.

To onlookers, we are a couple making out and nothing more. No one can see that he has his fingers inside me, slowly pushing in and out of my tight hole. It is the single most erotic moment of my life. It feels naughty, filthy even, and I love it.

He continues to move his fingers inside me, his thumb rubbing over that tight bundle of nerves that has the power to unravel me. I can feel my orgasm starting to build. My legs feel shaky and my chest is tight, as if someone is sitting on my ribs and stopping the air from pushing out of my lungs.

I lick my lips, trying to get some moisture back into my mouth as waves of pleasure start to build in my pelvis. I'm not going to last long. Not at this rate. I cling to him, as if he is lifesaving driftwood. He is all that's keeping me upright. I can't hear my pants over the music, which is just as well because I'm sure I would be making a fool of myself.

He kisses down my neck, touching the most sensitive part there and making me gasp. Then he moves to my ear. "Do you want me to fuck you, little dove?"

I do. I need to feel him stretching me. He's an addiction I can't get enough of. When he's inside me I feel powerful, different. I feel like an individual, and not just the daughter of

Declan Easton. I crave that feeling more than I've ever craved anything.

"Please fuck me," I moan out.

I have no idea if he can hear me over the music, but I don't care. I'm just focused on the sensations that are rolling through my pussy. Everything down there feels tight and contracted.

My thoughts scatter as I go over the edge, murmuring his name as I do. I lean forward, clinging to him so tightly I must be leaving bruises. He pulls his fingers out of me and moves them under his nose, as if sniffing them. Then he puts them in his mouth and sucks my juices off. My mouth dries. It shouldn't be hot, but it is.

When he kisses me, I can taste myself on his tongue.

He takes my hand in his. "Come and sit with me."

He moves me through the club, the crowd parting to let us pass and into the VIP area. He finds an empty booth. He sits first, letting me slip in behind him. His hand instantly goes back between my legs. I don't fight him. I don't have the strength to resist him any longer, and besides, the poor lighting at the table hides us from view. I want him to touch me. I need it. My pussy is pulsating, and I'm chasing that next high.

Pushing my thighs open, Luke tears my underwear, giving him complete access to between my legs. I could close them, but I don't. I wait in anticipation of what he's going to do. He strokes his fingers through my slit. I want to moan, but the music is lower in here and I don't want to make a scene.

"I missed you."

The admission surprises me because although I've been pining for him all week, needing his attention, I'm surprised he felt the same.

"I missed you too," I agree. I did. I am completely smitten with him. It is unsurprising really, considering the life I've lived. One without love or affection since the death of my mother. It seems obvious I would crave it anywhere I can find it, though I tell myself there is more than just need here. I want him.

"I want your number. I want to be able to contact you whenever I need you."

"I don't... have a phone." My words are breathy as he hits a particularly sensitive spot inside me. If he keeps this up, I'm going to come again.

"Make sure you have one next time you come here."

I want to ask him what I am to him, but it seems like that would be the wrong thing to do. He has not promised me anything, and I have not promised him anything either. Even if I wanted to, I can't. Luke is not my future, as much as I wish he could be.

I grip the edge of the table, my knuckles whitening as he brings me to orgasm again. It grows slowly in the pit of my pelvis before racing to the finish line. I duck my head, trying to breathe as paroxysmal waves wash over me. Luke might be the death of me. Death by orgasm sounds like a nice way to go.

He nuzzles my neck as I come down from my orgasm. "You're beautiful when you come," he says. His words heat my body, making me feel warm everywhere. He knows exactly what to say to make me feel special. "I don't understand why a girl like you would need to lose your virginity in the way you did."

I don't answer. What can I say? My father is making me marry a man who is old enough to be my grandfather? "It isn't a big deal."

"If it wasn't a big deal, then why didn't you just wait for the right person?"

"But I found the right person." It's cheesy to say, and I expect him to laugh at me, but he doesn't. Instead, he dips his head and takes my mouth again, pushing me back against the cushions of the booth. I can see the possession in his eyes as he peers down at me. He wants to own me, but not in the same way as Jeremiah. Luke wants me on a level playing field with him. He doesn't want me beneath him as a servant.

"Tell me about yourself, Alice."

"There is not much to tell."

"Do you work?"

I shake my head. For some reason this question embarrasses me. I should be able to take care of myself. I shouldn't have to rely on my father's money, but I do. I hate it. I hate relying on him for anything. It makes me feel more pathetic than I am.

"Tell me something about yourself."

"I miss my mother every day." I'm not sure what possesses me to say this, and to open up to him in this way, but the words come out of my mouth before I can stop them.

"Where is she?"

"She died when I was a child. It's just me and my father now."

Pain zings through my chest at the reminder of how alone I am. I live in a house with a monster who does not want me.

"Was she like you?"

I think about my mother and what I remember of her. The smile tugs on my lips. "She had a good heart, a kind soul. I try to live up to her every day, but I don't always succeed."

Luke stares at me for a beat, then he says, "Dance with me."

This surprises me so much I blink at him, not comprehending at first what he's asking. Before I can argue, he grabs my hand and pulls me out of the booth. Standing next to it, he takes my hand as he wraps his other one around my back, and we start to sway to the music. It's quieter in here, but there is still enough beat for me to sway my hips. I lean my head against his shoulder, feeling relaxed and at ease. He makes me feel safe, even though the reality couldn't be further from the truth. If my father found out Luke had taken my virginity, he would kill him. He might even kill me.

"I wish we could stay like this forever," I say in a soft voice.

Luke hears me. "So do I. But let's just enjoy the moment, little dove."

And that's exactly what I do. For a few hours I forget about my life, and I just enjoy good company and a brief moment of happiness.

CHAPTER 10

Sariah

L uke fills my head in the days after our meeting. In truth, he's all that keeps my head above water and stops me from drowning. Our time together had been a spot of light in an otherwise dark sky. He made me feel... alive.

He made me feel free.

I've been a prisoner in my own life for so long I forgot how it feels to have autonomy. It might be fleeting, but my fling with Luke is giving me a tantalising taste of normality. I'm tired of living in this cage.

I place my book on the end table with a sigh. I have barely read a word of it in the last hour. All I can think about is Luke. Every time I'm with him it's as if my world tilts on its axis. I find myself secretly smiling throughout the day as I remember things he said or did to me. It's a foolish childish dream, but I imagine us running away together. I envisage the life we would build together, free from syndicates and arranged marriages. But that is not to be my fate. I don't get the happily ever after. My life will always be dictated and my father will always have control over me.

The door opens to the living room and Declan steps inside. My heart instantly sinks.

If my mother still lived, she would not allow this marriage to take place. She would protect me from this monstrous act.

I have to go along with Declan's demands, no matter how much I hate it. It is the only way to remain safe, breathing, but Luke has ignited a little spark of rebellion inside me. I've had a taste of real chemistry and feelings. I want it. I want everything Luke offers—safety, security, and above all things, love.

What I have with him is addictive. I want desperately to pursue my relationship with Luke, but how can I? In less than two weeks I'll be saying my vows, binding myself to Jeremiah Wood.

How can I drag Luke into this hell?

"Wood is coming to see you tomorrow." Declan's words snap me out of my thoughts. Cold fills my belly at his words. Jeremiah is the last person I want to see. "Make sure you are presentable. We can't afford for him to back out of this wedding now. There's a lot riding on it."

I don't understand the intricacies and the inner workings of the syndicates that run London, but I know Declan is shoring up his power by joining me to the Woods. It is an alliance that will bring with it great benefits—for him, at least. I get nothing out of the deal.

Luke's face dances across my mind. I don't want to do this, and for the first time in my life, I feel strong enough to fight. I ball my hands into fists in my lap.

"I'm not marrying him." My words are soft, my voice trembling as I say them. I have never been so defiant, but I have to fight for my life, for the right to live it as I choose. This is my last chance.

Declan's eyes snap towards me, and I see the burn of fire within them. I've never stood up to him before. Not like this. "What the fuck did you say?" he hisses out. The anger that crackles through his voice makes shivers run up my spine.

"I don't want to marry him. You can't force me to. This isn't the fifteen hundreds. I have a say over my life."

I steel myself as the room seems to hold its breath. I hold my own as Declan stares at me through narrowed eyes. I can hardly draw air. My whole body feels tight and wired as I wait for him to respond to my words.

I expect his rage, so when he crosses the room towards me I come to my feet, ready to fight. It's self-preservation more than anything, a primal need to defend myself.

He stands in front of me, his dark eyes boring into mine, looking at me as if he can't believe my defiance. Probably he can't. I've always been the obedient servant.

Not anymore.

He grabs my arm in a bruising hold that makes me whimper. "You will do as you are told."

I peer up at him, seeing the monster in the forefront of his eyes. "You force me to do this, and I will tell the world you killed my mother."

It's a flame to a spark.

His hand wraps around my throat. The movement is so quick I barely register it until the air is cut off. My lungs stutter and my heart rate picks up its pace as I try to breathe.

Spittle collects at the corners of Declan's mouth, and his eyes are so wide I can see white encircling the irises completely. Terror climbs up my spine as he pushes me back onto the sofa. I go down hard as he comes down on top of me. His weight is so heavy it feels like a rock is sitting on my stomach.

I can't move and he hasn't released the pressure on my throat. I'm starting to feel weak, light-headed, even. Dark spots spill across my vision as I claw desperately at his hands wrapped around my neck.

Panic starts to infuse my body as I realise he is killing me. I am moments from death. My lungs burn now from lack of oxygen and my throat is raw. I desperately try to breathe, but nothing moves past his hands.

As I start to weaken, Luke drifts across my thoughts. I didn't think my life would be long or happy. I didn't expect to be taken out like this—the man who I called father most of my life squeezing the life out of me in the living room of the house I grew up in.

I stop fighting. My limbs are no longer cooperating anyway. I meet Declan's eyes and I make my peace with my end.

At least I managed to have something that was mine. I had a few magical nights with a man who wanted me for me, not because of what I could bring to the table. That means everything to me. Luke means everything to me.

Darkness creeps into the edge of my vision, shrouding the colours of the room in black. I'm close to passing out, hanging on by a thread to life.

The pressure on my throat is suddenly released. My body instinctively sucks in air, taking a huge gasping breath, chasing the blackness from my sight. Dizziness washes over me and my head rolls.

"See what you made me do," Declan hisses.

He lifts off me and paces the space in front of the sofa, raking his fingers through his hair as if I am a disobedient child who has dismayed him. That's precisely what I am. He thought I would just be the good girl doing everything she was told. He thought my fear would keep me paralysed, and maybe it would have if I hadn't met Luke.

For a moment, I just lie still, trying to drag air into my aching lungs and calm the roiling of my brain. I feel like I'm on the waltzers, spinning around and around. The room is moving.

I try to swallow, but my throat is burning. My stomach is churning and my body feels wrung out.

I sit up, my arms trembling as I do, and I rub at my burning throat. It's like shards of glass have been pushed down my windpipe.

I raise my eyes to find Declan's. "You can kill me, but I am not your puppet. Not anymore." My voice sounds ravaged, raw as if I have eaten razor blades. It feels like it too. No doubt I will wear a ring of bruises around my neck tomorrow.

If I make it to then.

My body is sluggish, my awareness slow, so I don't see his fist coming towards my face until it slams into my jaw with enough force to send me sprawling back amongst the sofa cushions.

My already dizzied head swims more from the blow, my ears ringing. My face burns and the skin already feels tight.

Declan grabs me by the hair, fisting his fingers into the roots and dragging me up. My scalp burns as if a thousand pins are stabbing into my head. I cry out in pain as I'm forced to my feet.

"You are just like your whore mother."

Those words hurt more than the assault that follows. His fists lash out, over and over, smashing into every part of my body. I try to protect myself, but I'm still weak from my near-death experience. I feel the anger, the rage in every punch, every hit he lands. He means to break me, and this time he just might.

I can feel blood on my face, warm, thick, and dripping. I don't know how it happened. It doesn't matter.

Declan grabs my bruised face between his fingers and forces me to look at him. The look in his eyes scares me. I've seen him lose control before, but this is something else. It's like the lights are on, but he's checked out completely. The beast within him has come out to play.

"If you ever threaten me again, I will end your fucking life."

He releases me with a hard shove. I sprawl backwards, my body unable to hold itself together any longer. I can smell the wood floor beneath me, the scent infusing my nose as I lay against it, unable to move.

I hate myself for lying there, helpless and pathetic, broken and bruised.

The sound of the door opening and then slamming shut makes me jolt. I'm alone. It's only then I let my tears fall. I've never felt so desperate in my life. This can't be my path.

But he will never let me go, and Jeremiah will claim what he owns. I want to have the fairy-tale ending where Luke and I ride off into the sunset, but reality doesn't work like that.

I can't drag him into this mess. Declan would kill him for touching me, and he doesn't deserve that. No, this cross is mine alone to bear, and I won't drag an innocent man into this. What Luke and I had was good, but it's done. It has to be.

My trembling fingers move over my lips, and I taste blood on them. Crimson droplets stain the wood beneath me, sinking into the grain. A tactile reminder of what happened here.

I don't move for a long time. I just keep still and focus on trying to breathe through the pain, but I know I eventually need to get up. If Declan comes back and finds me where he left me, he'll beat me again—worse.

I push carefully up to my knees. I can't stop the cry from escaping my mouth as I move. White hot pain lances through my chest, causing me to gasp.

Fuck.

Every inch of my body is on fire. I've never felt anything like this before. It is not the first beating I've taken from him, but this is the worst. It feels like something is broken inside me. My ribs ache as I move, and I gasp out a breath as I manage to move to the edge of the sofa.

"What did you do, Declan?" I whimper.

I manage to hoist myself onto the sofa. I lean carefully back against the cushions, holding my ribs as I do. It relieves a little of the pressure, though not enough. Every movement is fire.

Declan wanted to kill me. It's a hard truth to realise, but he meant to end my life. I felt it in the anger of his attack.

Why am I still breathing?

Because I am promised to Jeremiah, and Declan won't break that deal. That is all that stayed his hand. He is a monster who wants to ruin me for his own benefit. He can try, but I will make it my mission to bring him down for the death of my mother.

CHAPTER 11

Lucas

Alice isn't at Tease on Friday night, and Granger's having little luck discovering who she is. Both things irritate me. I want to know who Alice really is, and the lack of information is starting to piss me off. It's like she's a ghost, but everyone has a footprint. Granger just has to find it.

It's Saturday morning—now comes the hangover. When Alice didn't turn up, I drank more than my share of scotch at the bar. I'd had plenty of women wanting to come home with me, but I brushed them all off.

Perhaps it is a good thing she didn't show up. She and I can never be together. I have no idea who I'm promised to, but I do know I can never be with Alice. No matter how much I want to be. For my family, I will marry someone who will further our cause. I've known that would be my destiny from the moment I was old enough to understand marriage.

"We have to move quickly," my mother says. I have no idea what we are moving quickly to as I haven't been listening. I glance around the boardroom table, trying to get some notion of what might have been said, but my father Anthony shows nothing on his face. Zeke looks annoyed, but that's not unusual when he's dealing with our parents. Kane, on the other hand, looks fucking homicidal.

I sit up straighter, tuning into the conversation and realising I might actually need to pay attention.

"What does marrying Kane to the Adams bitch achieve?" Zeke demands. "They are already our allies without chaining him to them."

I understand now why Kane looks close to murdering our mother. He will marry her for the greater good of the family, but it doesn't mean he is happy about the fact. None of us wish to have our wives chosen for us.

Zeke is lucky he found Bailey and that it was a marriage our parents approved of, though I suspect he would not have given up Bailey for any reason. Not even his family. I understand that, now that I have had Alice. The intensity of something so pure in my world has surprised even me. It's hard to ignore it when your heart is telling you to grab hold of someone with two hands and hold on for dear life.

"You know what it will achieve, Zeke. Don't be so obtuse. It will protect us and offer a buffer. The Adams's are far less likely to attack if we have one of the daughters."

I watch as my mother twirls a strand of blonde hair between her fingers. On the surface, Charlotte Fraser looks like a vapid empty-headed bimbo. It couldn't be further from the truth. Most of the things that happen within our family are orchestrated by her.

"I'm also looking for someone for you, Lucas."

My head snaps up at that. I'm twenty-two, and I'm certainly not ready for a wife yet. "Well, look elsewhere. I'm not interested in whatever plot you're concocting."

Charlotte scowls at me like I'm a wayward child and not a grown man who was murdered more people than I can count. My hands are covered in the blood of my victims, and yet I am a slave to my parents' demands. This isn't about any one of us—it's about keeping our family on top. That allows us to keep Aurelia safe, and that is all I care about.

"Don't be difficult," Charlotte says, her hand coming to her forehead as if she's getting a headache. "Your brother is already making things hard."

"I don't want to marry the Adams bitch," Kane says.

"No one wants to enter into an arranged marriage, Kane, but your family needs you to do this. I'm worried about the Eastons consolidating their power with the North. It can't happen. We must safeguard against future attacks. We need to find a way to stop this wedding between Jeremiah Wood and Sariah Easton."

"And how do you propose to do that?" Zeke asks.

Anthony pushes up from his chair and moves to the window. It runs the whole length of the room, overlooking the London skyline. There is also a wall of windows facing into the office. Usually, the cubicles on the other side would be filled with employees, but it's late and everyone has gone home, apart from Talia. My father's assistant is always on hand in case he requires anything. "We stop the wedding, and we marry your sister to Jeremiah Wood."

Kane shoots to his feet, slamming his palms against the desk. "Absolutely fucking not."

My father has always been a cunt. He and my mother ruined our childhoods. They created many soldiers who would continue the legacy. I respect my father's position because it keeps me and my siblings safe, but I would usurp my father and put Kane on his throne in a heartbeat if I thought we could get away with it. As much as I despise my parents, they have the support of our men. They are loyal, and they would not follow us if we betrayed Anthony.

Charlotte drops a hand to her hip as she stares down Kane's defiance. "Why not?"

"Wood has a reputation for being, shall we say, less than

savoury," Zeke answers instead of Kane. His lips pull into the disgusted snarl.

"That's putting it mildly," Kane snaps. "You're not subjecting our sister to a cunt like that."

Charlotte throws her hands the air, frustrated tension rolling through her shoulders. "How did I raise such disobedient children?"

I want to point out that Charlotte didn't raise us. She trained us. We were soldiers before we were children. We each had our role to play, and still do, but that brought us closer together as siblings. There is nothing I would not do for Zeke, Kane, or Aurelia. Our parents cemented an alliance that was unbreakable between the four of us. I don't believe that was their intention, but my brothers and sister are the only people I trust.

Wood is known for his cruelty, and while I have no feelings about the Easton woman marrying him, my sister going to that fate makes my jaw tight. I will protect Aurelia. "Come up with a new plan," I tell my mother.

"The only other plan is for you to marry the Easton girl, or your sister marries Wood. What other choice is there, Lucas?"

I have no desire to marry Sariah Easton, not now I have feelings for Alice, but I'll not push my sister into a marriage with a monster. I have to make a split-second decision. Doom my sister to a life of misery or take this bullet for her. I choose the latter. Aurelia is barely eighteen. She deserves some chance at life before she's tied down.

"Fine." I will take that burden from my sister. I have power in a relationship that Aurelia does not.

Charlotte turns to Kane. "Why can't you be more like your brother?"

Kane glares at her with the heat of a thousand fires. "I didn't say I wouldn't do it. Just that I didn't want to."

"If we can marry Kane into the Adams syndicate and

Lucas into the Easton family, we'll be surrounded by allies," Anthony says as he shoves his fists into his suit trouser pockets.

I try to ignore the empty feeling in my gut as my parents discuss the finer points of how to release Sariah Easton from her current betrothal. I feel all my control slipping through my fingers, and I hate it. As usual, though, I have to play the good little soldier.

"You know Wood will never allow this to happen." Zeke drums his fingers on the table. "Trying to undercut him is going to result in a war between us and the Manchester syndicates."

Zeke is right. Jeremiah will have to attack us to save face. Otherwise, he's going to look like a weak prick. He is not going to want that to happen.

"Then what do you propose?" Charlotte demands. I can hear the irritation in her voice. Our questioning is pissing her off. Our mother is not a woman who's used to having her plans scrutinised so deeply. "That we just allow them to consolidate their power? We might as well offer them an open invitation to take over our territory."

Zeke shifts his shoulders. I can tell he's getting irritated by the conversation.

You and me both, brother.

"All I know is, if you do this, you open us to up problems down the road."

"But if we have the support of both syndicates and the Untamed Sons...," Charlotte trails off, using her hands as scales, as if she's weighing up the pros and cons. Neither exists. There are only winners and losers. The only thing we can do is make sure we end up on the right side of the win.

"And when they retaliate?" I ask.

It's playing with fire. Even though our counterproposal may be more appealing than Jeremiah Wood's, it doesn't mean Declan Easton will break his deal and hand his daughter over to me. My mother is fucking deluded if she thinks that's going to happen.

But Charlotte isn't someone who likes to hear the word no. She has a plan, and I know my mother. She will not stop until she has enacted it. Charlotte wants me married to Sariah. It suits her narrative, and it would help shore up our defences against an Easton/Wood alliance. Particularly if Kane goes ahead with this proposal to wed one of the Adams's. Fuck, I get sick of the politics, of all the manoeuvring and conniving. I hate it, even if I understand why it has to happen.

"They won't. Besides—" Charlotte waves her hand. "— why would Declan Easton refuse our proposal? We are powerful, and he knows that. More so than the fucking Woods. Why would he choose such a weak alliance when he can have the strength of the Fraser family behind him?"

"For arguments sake," I say, "let's just imagine Declan Easton may have some scruples and decide to keep the deal he has in place. What then, Mother?"

She glares at me as if I've lost my mind. "But that's not going to happen, darling, is it?"

That she believes in her own hype only serves to concern me. We are not as strong as she thinks, because if we were, she wouldn't care about this alliance. The fact that it has her and Anthony worried tells me everything.

"I'll talk to Declan, and I'll see what he says. I'm very persuasive when I have to be." She is very persuasive full stop. "The wedding is meant to take place in two weeks' time. That gives us opportunity to lay the foundation. I have a registrar who can fudge the paperwork. It would normally take twenty-eight days, but we won't want to wait that long."

I ignore the churning in my gut at her words. If my mother gets her way, in two weeks' time I will have a woman who I call wife. A woman I've never met before or even laid eyes on.

Fuck.

I turn to Kane and give him a wry smile. "It looks like we are going to have a double wedding on the horizon."

The look Kane gives me could melt the polar ice caps. My brother never has had much of a sense of humour.

I rap my knuckles on the desk and push up to my feet. I'm bored of this conversation and where it's going. "Just tell me where I need to be and when."

As I step out of the boardroom and make my way down the corridor towards the exit, I find Aurelia sitting in one of the chairs near the lift. My sister is stunningly beautiful, something she got from our mother. Charlotte may be poison, but she looks like an angel. It's that deception that draws people into her and gets them killed.

"What are you doing here?" I ask, going over to her quickly. She looks unharmed. In fact, she's wearing high heels and a dark-coloured dress.

She rolls her eyes at me, flicking her dark hair over her shoulder. "Mum called me an hour ago and asked me to meet her here."

"You didn't come alone, did you?" My heart stutters at the thought. Aurelia is a prime target for abduction by our enemies.

"Aaron brought me."

Aaron Leep is one of my father's lieutenants, but he has recently been assigned to my sister's protection detail because he could be trusted. I'm thinking that faith might have been misplaced, considering there's no fucking sign of him.

"And where is the prick?" He's not supposed to leave her fucking side. I grate my teeth and clench my jaw.

"Relax. He's down in the lobby. I hardly need protection here, Luke."

Luke....

That name has always been one given to me by my family, but now it just reminds me of Alice. I love the way it sounds on her lips when I'm inside her. Fuck. I need to find her. I need to see her again and experience the highs she gives me when we are together. She's like a natural drug. One I can't get enough of.

"You are being careful, aren't you?"

My heart stutters a little at the thought she might be taking risks, giving Aaron the runaround. I know what it's like to be young and wanting to experience freedom. I was given that opportunity, but Aurelia will never have it. It's too dangerous to allow her off the reins. She is our weakest link, the thing that can be used against us to hurt our empire. I'm not sure if she understands how much sway she holds over her siblings. It would break the three of us if anything happened to her.

"Don't worry. Your little guard has kept me locked up tight."

At least Aaron is doing that part of his job well.

"Don't take any risks."

She peers up at me, her brows drawing together. "Is something happening?"

Something is always happening, but I don't tell her that. I don't want her to ever be scared. Everything we do is to ensure the survival of the family so that Aurelia can have a good life. I lean down and kiss her head, smelling her shampoo and her perfume. It is a scent that is so familiar, so her, that it makes me smile. "Nothing at all," I lie. If she knows our mother is orchestrating two weddings behind the scenes, it will only upset her. "Be careful with Charlotte. She is in a meddling mood."

Aurelia rolls her eyes. "When isn't she?"

My sister's right, so I just laugh as I make my way to the

lift, giving my sister a wave before I push the button to call it to the floor. I'm not particularly keen to make someone my wife, but like my brothers, I will do what I must to protect the Fraser name—even if it means marrying a total stranger. Two weeks ago that would have been easy, but now a certain blonde angel commands my thoughts, and I find myself wishing life was different and that she could be mine.

The desire is a foolish want, and one I can't have. It's time to put Alice out of my mind and focus on the future with Sariah Easton because if I know one thing about my mother, it's that she will always get her way. So I will marry the Easton girl, no matter my thoughts on it.

CHAPTER 12

Sariah

My ribs ache fiercely as I try to sit up straight. I know Declan will be angry if I slouch. I can't hide the bruises on my face. They are there for everyone to see. If I expect Jeremiah to care that my father beat me, I'm sorely mistaken. The man has been sitting opposite me for the last hour, staring at me like I'm a prize he's won. From the little smirk he keeps making, I surmise he is pleased by my father's show of discipline.

"What did you do to warrant such a beating?" he asks. "I don't like disobedience."

I feel like I'm shrivelling inside myself. How can this be my fate? I should be sobbing, weeping for the future that lies ahead of me, but I feel numb. Empty. What does it matter what happens to me? I have no voice left. No ability to grow into the person I should be.

Whoever that is.

I sit demurely, not daring to breathe or move in case I anger somebody. I feel beaten down, and I hate the person I am becoming. This is not who I am, but what do I have left to fight for? A path that has been chosen for me. A husband who will abuse me as much as my father has. A life I did not want.

I want to tell Jeremiah I don't want him, but a glare from Declan holds my tongue. My fingers move absently to my wrist where the missing bracelet usually sits. I think I must have left it in the hotel room, and it breaks my heart. It was my mother's. I have other trinkets of hers so it's not the only thing I have left, but I feel its loss like a physical blow.

"You know how these girls can be," Declan says, speaking for me. "Sometimes a heavy hand is needed to keep them in line."

Jeremiah leans back in his seat and eyes me. "Discipline is important."

Loathing rolls through every cell in my body. I despise this man. The thought of being in his clutches for the rest of my natural born life makes my stomach roll. Maybe I can run away. Start a new life somewhere else.

With what money?

I try to ignore that voice in the back of my head that taunts me. It makes me feel useless and pathetic. As much as I hate to admit it to myself, I am both.

"I find a good beating now and again makes all the difference," Declan says, keeping his attention locked on me. I can see his eyes are silently communicating that if I don't toe the line, he will hurt me again. I'm not sure how much more I can take. He's already hurt me so much.

"I'm looking forward to the wedding, my dear," Jeremiah says.

Nausea rolls up my throat at the thought of it. Even so I managed to choke out a "Me too."

I hate myself saying those words and going along with this horrific plan. I wish I could channel my mother's strength. I wish I could stand up for myself and be the hero of my own story. I had tried that, and it didn't end well. My ribs throb as if to remind me of the pain I suffered for my show of defiance.

Jeremiah pushes up from his seat and comes to sit next to me. I try not to stiffen as he moves so close to me our legs are touching. He reaches out and runs his fingers through the ends of my hair, skimming over the top of my breast as he does. I will myself to stay calm. "You have no idea how lucky you are, darling."

It doesn't have the same impact on me as when Luke calls me his little dove. There is something sinister behind Jeremiah's endearment. When Luke says his words to me, I feel cherished.

"I'm going to make you my queen. You'll sit at my side. Looking like a pretty little ornament. And you are pretty, my dear. Like a porcelain doll. You have your mother's look about you."

It's the first thing he's said to me that elicits a response. My mother being on his tongue infuriates me. He doesn't have the right to say her name to me.

It also gains a response from Declan. His jaw clenches and I see the annoyance at having her brought up. He will never get over what she did to him. Even though he made her pay the ultimate price for her mistake.

If it was a mistake.

I have no idea if my mother loved my real father. Knowing how it feels to be trapped in a relationship not of your choosing, I can understand why she might have found sanctuary in the arms of another. I didn't understand it for a long time. Meeting Luke changed that. I've tasted what a real relationship could feel like.

"There is not much of you in her, Declan," Jeremiah mocks. He means it is a joke, but it hits too close to that raw nerve that Declan has exposed.

"Alice was far prettier than I am, so it's just as well Sariah takes after her mother."

Jeremiah leans into me and presses his mouth against the side of my cheek. I hold still, frozen. I'm not scared. I just feel helpless.

The touch of his mouth against my skin makes me crawl inside myself. He leans into me and speaks directly into my ear. "I will expect you to be an obedient wife. You won't want to cross me."

"Sariah, excuse us for a moment. I need to talk to Jeremiah alone."

Grateful for the reprieve, I push up from my seat and have to stop myself from running to the door. As soon as I'm on the other side of it and it shuts behind me, I let my tears fall. I can't do this. I can't be strong. I feel like I'm coming apart at the seams. Every conversation with Jeremiah rips my soul to shreds. I should move away from the door, but I find myself lingering there. Listening will get me worse than a beating. I know it, but I still press my ear back against the door frame.

"... better offer, don't you think?" Declan says.

There's a pause, then Jeremiah responds. "If it's about money, we can come to an arrangement."

"I have money, Wood. It's about what you're bringing to the table. The Frasers are powerful, and having them onside—"

"And what makes you think I'm not powerful?" The bite in Jeremiah's voice scares me. I've never heard him speak like this during his visits. I can tell he's angry, but his words are given calmly, something Declan has never mastered.

"I don't deny your strength. You still don't have the sway they do. If I'm going to go against Charlotte fucking Fraser, I want assurances. She didn't beat around the bush. If I don't marry my daughter to her son, there will be consequences.

I'm willing to face those if I have your word you will stand with me against them."

My heart starts to pound against my ribs. Declan really sees me as a bargaining chip, a thing he can just palm off to suit his needs. I've never felt so dehumanised in all my life. I know he hates me because of my mother's infidelity, but I never realised until this moment how much. He would just sell me to the highest bidder.

Everyone knows about the Frasers. They are another crime family who, like my father, own a slice of London. Their reputation precedes them. I've heard of Charlotte and Anthony, the heads of the family, and Kane, the eldest son. But that's all I know. Is it Kane Charlotte means to marry me to? From what I hear, he is no different from Jeremiah, and I am no more inclined to marry him than I am the man sitting behind the door I'm listening at.

"You have my word. Charlotte Fraser and those cunt sons of hers think they own the city. With my support they will see how wrong they are. Declan, you have the strength to take them down. Once the Frasers fall, there is only the Adams syndicate standing in our way. We'll crush both of them."

"Charlotte isn't going to go away easily," Declan says. "That bitch doesn't like hearing the word no. It will mean war."

"If you don't give me your fucking daughter, you will have war with the Woods. The Fraser pricks are not the only ones you should fear."

I hear shuffling and realise he is moving around. I can't move fast because of my injuries, so I slip into adjacent room, which happens to be a small library. I close the door quietly, pressing my hand against the wood to act as a brace to stop it from squeaking. I leave a small gap, just enough to see the hallway beyond, so when Jeremiah steps out of the room, I see a flash of colour as he storms away.

I hold my breath until I hear my father pass by as well. Then I make my way back to my bedroom with my mind in turmoil. Declan is going to sell me off to the highest bidder, and I will have no choice in the matter.

CHAPTER 13

Lucas

"**D**eclan Easton refused our marriage proposal." Charlotte bangs her fist down on the table as she paces the boardroom. It's been a week since the initial idea was presented to me, and clearly my mother's negotiations have failed miserably. Though I doubt she did much in the way of compromise. Charlotte Fraser is not known for that. I'm not sure why she's surprised, but her anger doesn't shock me. I figured this would be the outcome and that she would be annoyed when things didn't go the way she wanted.

Despite what my mother thinks, she can't control everything. I've been thinking a lot lately about Alice and the life we could have had if I wasn't who I am. I don't despise my life. I have money, means, and a thirst for blood that is quenched by my work, but there is something missing. I wonder what it would be like to just meet someone in a club as I did Alice and have a normal relationship with them, one that isn't part of the political game.

Granger didn't manage to find anything out about her, which surprised the fuck out of me. It's like Alice doesn't have a footprint, or at least not a digital one. There are no social media pictures of her, and she's not searchable in the usual places. It stumped the fuck out of Granger. He's never met a challenge he can't unpick—until Alice. With no leads, I've given up hope of ever seeing her again. She hasn't been to the club again, so I have to let her go, as much as I don't want to.

Zeke is sitting next to me, his expression tight. He's pissed because he had to come to this meeting. He and Bailey are supposed to be going out for dinner, and he's annoyed he's had to stand her up for this. Kane is sitting opposite us on the other side of the table, next to Anthony.

Charlotte paces the floor in front of the table, the carpet softening the clack of her skyscraper-high heels. I don't think I've ever seen my mother in flats. I'm not even convinced she owns any. She pushes her suit jacket back as she drops her hands to her hips. The flowy blouse she's wearing is no doubt high quality and expensive. Charlotte doesn't do off-the-rack. My father joked that she bankrupts him with her shopping escapades. If he had any sense, he'd take the credit cards off her. She would probably murder him in his sleep if he did, so I understand why he allows her spending sprees.

"Who gives a fuck what the Easton cunt does," Kane snarls. His patience is thin lately, which makes me wonder how far Charlotte has got with plans for his wedding.

"I do, and you should too. This is your family on the line. At least pretend you care."

Kane sits up straight in his seat, and I see the moment his control snaps. "I've done everything this family has asked of me and more. Don't sit there and pretend I haven't."

"So, what is your plan now, Mother?" Zeke asks, cutting through the tension before Kane can commit matricide."

Charlotte gives her attention to Zeke. "We can't allow the wedding to go ahead. It threatens our security and creates an enemy capable of taking us down. We have to stop it."

I cock my brow and glance at my father. Surely he's not on

board with such a reckless plan? When he doesn't speak or try to talk Charlotte down, I can't stop myself from questioning his judgement. "Are you listening to this madness?" I demand.

"I agree with your mother." Anthony leans back, lacing his fingers over his stomach. "We have to nip this in the bud, and the way to do that is to marry you to the Easton girl. Willing or not. That way Wood can't have her."

I glance up at the ceiling and ask the universe for patience. "You want to steal this girl and make her marry me?" The idea does not sit well with me. An arranged marriage is one thing. Both parties are aware of what is happening—but to sneak her off somewhere and just force her into it is wrong. "You can't even get married that fast in this country. You have to give a months' notice."

Charlotte waves this off. "I told you before, I know someone who can fudge the documentation. I can have you married in an afternoon if I wish."

Sometimes her reach scares me. Not to mention the lengths she will go to in order to further our family name.

"There is a small snag in your plan," Zeke says. "Sariah Easton is hidden away. How precisely do you intend to prevent the wedding and bring her to Luke?"

"We can't do it at the wedding itself. There will be too many people there. Two crime families joining together equals a lot of firepower. I don't intend on letting anyone die doing this. But I do happen to know Little Miss Easton will be travelling to the church at precisely 10:05 in the morning. Now, if we were to intercept her car, we could have her brought to Lucas instead of to Jeremiah Wood. It's still risky as she'll have security, though there will be less of it on the road than there will be at the church. That's going to be our only option."

It's not a bad plan, considering the alternatives, but it's

still ridiculous. Charlotte comes to stand behind my father, dropping her hand on his shoulder. Anthony reaches up and places his hand over hers, giving it a gentle squeeze. I can see the pride in his face at what he thinks is my mother's genius.

"And what happens when Easton and Wood find their darling Sariah missing?" Zeke demands. It's a fair question, because I can guarantee neither party is going to take this lying down.

"That is the whole reason we are planning to marry Kane to the Adams girl. Her father has agreed to that match. Next month Kane will marry his eldest daughter, Elena."

Kane sits up straight in his seat. He had expected this, no doubt, but it's about to become his reality. That has to be an unsettling thought, because I also feel so unsettled right now.

"It's too bad we couldn't have a double wedding," Charlotte says, twirling her hair almost whimsically. She doesn't look like a master manipulator right now, even though that's precisely what she is. "The timing just won't allow it. Hamish wants a full event for his daughter, and I can't say I blame him. We've agreed to pay most of the costs, so no expense will be spared."

I can only imagine how ostentatious it will be. Charlotte turns to me. "Unfortunately, darling, I don't think you're going to get the same elaborate affair."

Does she really think I give a fuck about a big fancy wedding? I don't even want to marry this woman. She can be dressed in a sack for all I'd notice.

"There isn't going to be time," my mother continues, "but perhaps we can have a party once the dust settles."

If the dust settles.

I believe that, as usual, my mother has underestimated how pissed off everyone is going to be by her actions. Charlotte Fraser will do what she wants, and the rest of us will just have to hold on for the ride.

"And what if the girl says no? What then? No one is ever going to marry someone against their will, no matter how much you pay them."

"Oh, she'll marry you. It'll be a legally binding agreement, Lucas. Don't worry about that. As for the girl, she's a means to an end, so it doesn't matter if you love her or even like her. If you don't marry her, the alternative is to kill her. Take her out of the picture. I thought I showed great reserve with this course of action."

While I have no feelings towards the girl, and it's no skin off my nose if she is dead, we don't harm innocents.

My stomach feels hollow. I knew this day would come, but now that it's here and real, I'm not sure I can face it. Alice sweeps across my memory once more, and I mourn for the relationship we could have had if our lives had been normal. But normal isn't a word I know because I was born a Fraser, and I have to do my duty to my family.

And I will.

"Tell me the plan."

Charlotte grins and moves to the chair at the head of the table. She then lays out the details of how we are going to snatch Sariah Easton so I can marry her instead of Jeremiah Wood.

CHAPTER 14

Sariah

I n the lead-up to the wedding I feel nauseous, like my belly is a stormy sea. Clinging to my memories of Luke is all that gets me through. It's his face I see when I try on my wedding dress. It's his hands I feel when Jeremiah touches me. It's his voice I hear when my father snarls terrible curses at me.

I exist in a daze, trying not to count down the days to my doom. At least I know I will go to my wedding bed having experienced the gentle touch of the man I wanted. I do not think Jeremiah will seek to pleasure me in the same way Luke did.

As always when I think about him, my face relaxes and I feel at ease. In my dreams I imagine I run away with Luke, and we start a new life far from Declan's reach. I consider running more than once, but my fear keeps me trodden down, unable to bring myself to do what is necessary. Declan also increases my guards, making it impossible to sneak out. They stand sentry outside my room and underneath my window. I can barely take a bathroom break without someone watching the door. I am more of a prisoner than I have ever been. The little dove has had her wings ripped off.

I hate it.

I feel alone and helpless. I hate myself for not fighting, but I have no fight left to give.

On the day of the wedding, I spend the first half hour of the morning in the bathroom puking my guts up. Unease slithers across my skin as I think about what is coming. I can't do this. I'm not strong enough.

I want to hide in my bedroom all day, but the wedding planner comes to get me dressed. If she notices I'm barely keeping it together, she doesn't show it. She busies herself around making sure my hair and make-up are perfect. At any other time, I might enjoy this pampering. Right now, it just feels like I have shackles around my wrists moving me closer to a fate I do not want. I don't pretend to be happy. I can't.

As I stare at myself in the mirror hanging over my dressing table, my make-up pristine over my face, I don't recognise the woman staring back at me. Dark eyes, fake lashes, rosy cheeks, my hair piled in curls on top of my head. I look beautiful, more perfect than I've ever looked in my life.

I'm a doll.

They dressed me up and painted my face on, hiding the bruises my father had given me, but they can't hide the sadness in my eyes. Nothing can hide that. I peer at my white gown. The bodice is exquisite, inlaid with pearls and beads that shimmer in the light. The sweetheart neckline accentuates my shoulders and neck, giving me the appearance of a swan. The skirts are huge and fluffy, and they engulf most of the stool I'm sitting on, which has disappeared beneath the sea of taffeta and lace.

"Just the veil now, Sariah," the wedding planner says. "You do make a beautiful bride."

I lower my gaze from the mirror, not wanting to look at myself any longer. The wedding planner moves behind me and places my veil on the back of my head. She flips the heavy lace over my face, shrouding me from the world. It feels hot as my breath has nowhere to go. Did they choose this veil on purpose so the guests in the church won't see my tears? At least not until the final moment, when Jeremiah is allowed to lift it so he can kiss me after we've been pronounced man and wife.

"The car is waiting for you."

It might as well be a hearse taking me to my own funeral.

I stand slowly, adjusting to the weight of the dress, and I lift the skirts so I can step into beautiful white heels with diamonds on the front. I smooth my dress down and stare at the door. Then I blow out a breath and follow the wedding planner out of the room.

It's difficult to navigate the stairs and she has to help me, lifting the back of my dress so I don't trip. Part of me wishes I would. Maybe then the wedding would be called off.

No such luck. I make it to the bottom unhindered.

Declan is waiting by the door, dressed in his suit with his hair slicked back and smart. He doesn't look at me like the doting father. There is no pride or joy in his eyes. He drags a critical gaze over me and must find me satisfactory because he moves out of the house towards the shiny black car that is waiting outside.

The wedding planner helps me into the vehicle, pushing my dress into the footwell and closing the door behind me. I feel like I'm suffocating with the amount of lace surrounding me, and I close my eyes behind the veil, hoping Declan can't see me breaking down internally.

I keep Luke's face in my mind, and it helps slow my breathing. In less than an hour's time I will be Mrs Sariah Wood. The name doesn't fit me. It's like a jigsaw piece that has been forced into the wrong slot.

My father doesn't speak as the car moves up the driveway towards the main gate of the house. He doesn't say a word to me until halfway to the church when he tells me, "You will find some happiness with him."

I'm not sure if he's feeling guilty for what he's doing as the realisation sets in that he is selling me to this man. His words surprise me though.

I stare out of the side window through my veil, watching the world pass me by in a blur of motion. "What do you care if I'm happy?"

"I believed you were my daughter for a long time, Sariah." He says as if that excuses his behaviour—as if it fixes everything he's done.

I turn to face him, and I let my anger seep into my words. "And yet you'd sell me to a man I don't want. You've never seen me as your daughter from the moment you learned about my mother's infidelity." Declan flinches as if I've struck him. Then he steels his jaw, and I think he's going to grab me by the face, but instead he just crosses his hands in his lap.

"I hope you never love someone as deeply as I loved your mother," he says, his voice soft but laced with hurt. "Her affair destroyed me. She gutted me and ripped out my heart when I learnt you weren't mine. Do you have any idea what it's like to think you are a father and then learn the child you doted on is nothing to do with you?"

"The difference is, Declan, I would never have taken that out on the child. What happened wasn't my fault."

"You look like her." His eyes go to the window as he speaks. "I couldn't bear looking at you after what she did. I still can't."

"Then why didn't you let me go? I could have had a life that was different and that was my own."

"I couldn't deal with the shame of people knowing your mother stepped out on me."

This admission doesn't surprise me, though it is upsetting.

"It's not too late to stop this."

"I'm afraid it is, Sariah. I made a deal with Jeremiah, and I'm not going to go back on it."

I turn away, unable to look at him. He disgusts me. "At least tell me this: who is my real father?"

He doesn't answer. I hate him for that. I excuse most of his other behaviour, overlook it even, but for him to deny me the chance to meet the man who created me and gave me life infuriates me.

"Fuck you," I hiss under my breath. "Fuck you, Declan Easton."

He starts to respond, but the car jerks suddenly and the brakes are slammed on. I throw my hands out as I'm catapulted into the back of the seat in front of me. My shoulder aches from the impact, but I'm not hurt. The car goes still, and I can hear raised voices outside the vehicle. My heart starts to pound as I glance around quickly, desperately trying to see what is going on. The security window between the driver and the back seat is up and blacked out so I can't see the road in front of the car, and there is nothing to see through the side windows.

"What the fuck is going on?" Declan demands of the driver, but before anyone can respond, a *rat-tat-tat* sound fills the air, and I hear the smashing of glass as the car rocks slightly.

Gunfire.

That sound is gunfire.

We are being shot at. Declan understands this faster than I do and already has a gun out. My eyes flare. He came armed to the church?

The door is suddenly torn open on Declan's side, and a gun is shoved in his face before he can respond with his own. I don't see what happens because my own door is dragged open. I turn my head, and as I do, I find myself looking down the barrel of a very nasty-looking gun. Terror claws up my spine, and the back of my neck suddenly feels clammy. I raise my eyes slowly to the figure holding the weapon. He is wearing a ski mask, and all I can see are hard eyes staring back at me.

"Do you have any idea who the fuck I am?" Declan snarls.

"Know who you are. Don't give a fuck." The voice that speaks is deep and gravelly. It's also filled with cold detachment that makes my body feel like it's been doused in ice.

The man on my side pushes the gun further into my field of vision. "Out."

I'm frozen in fear. I couldn't move even if I wanted to.

On the other side of me, the gun goes off and Declan cries out. I twist around and see the blood pouring from between his fingers as he clutches his shoulder.

"Out of the car or he'll shoot him again," the man standing next to me says. I don't really care what he does to Declan, but I'd rather not have my own brains splattered over the back of the car.

It takes me far too long to get out of the vehicle with all my skirts and train. The man holding the gun on me doesn't help, but he does grab my arm as soon as I'm free of the car and all but drags me over to a black 4x4.

The masked man shoves my dress into the car after me and slams the door. My heart is hammering. I always knew as the daughter of a high-ranking crime boss I could be taken and used against my father. If this is their plan, they are deluded. Declan will never pay to have me back. He doesn't care about me in any way other than ones that benefit him.

The door on the opposite side of the car opens, and a man in a ski mask climbs in. The man who is holding the gun on me gets into the front, and then the car tears out of there.

I try to keep myself calm and collected, but my mind is racing. Who are these men? And what are they going to do to me?

I turn to the man sitting next to me with his ski mask still in place, and I try not to let my fear seep into my voice when I ask, "Who are you?"

I can barely breathe beneath the veil and I'm not sure how much of my face he can see beneath the thick lace, but his eyes find mine, dark pits that are like staring into an abyss.

"Your worst nightmare."

CHAPTER 15

Lucas

I'm not nervous, but I feel uneasy as I wait for my father's men to return with Sariah Easton. I'm not sure I'm ready for this. I wait in the back of the small chapel with the priest who is ready to marry us. I've no idea where my mother found this man, but he seems nervous and on edge. I don't blame him. Our family has that effect on people.

Charlotte is sitting in the front pew with Anthony and Aurelia. Zeke and Kane are in the row behind, suited and booted. I'm surprised my sister was allowed to come, considering the shitstorm that might be brought down because of this, but Charlotte seems determined to have as normal a wedding as possible. As if this is some grand family affair. She is fucking crazy.

I readjust the arm of my suit jacket, counting down the minutes until I lose my freedom. I hate my mother for putting me in this position, even if I understand why she would think this is the best course of action. Charlotte has always been about desperate measures, no matter the consequences. I just hope this one doesn't backfire on us.

"Lucas, come and sit down." Charlotte gestures at me to join them at the front of the chapel, but I don't move. The thought of being in the same vicinity as that woman right now makes me want to commit an atrocity.

"I'm fine where I am." I return my attention to the open door that leads out to the front of the church. I want to see the car coming. I want to see her before everyone else does. I don't know why it matters, but for some reason it is important to me.

Kane stands and comes towards me. As always, my brother's expression is grim. He stops in front of me, his own eyes looking out the door. "There is still time to run," he says.

"And miss this?"

"We could just kill her."

Trust Kane to go right to violence. "Charlotte, or my wife-to-be?"

"I'm open to either."

I snort and shake my head. "The girl's innocent. Her only crime is being born into this world."

"You're going to tell Charlotte to shove it, then?" He looks positively giddy at the prospect.

"Our family needs this, Kane. I'll do what is necessary to keep us all safe." My gaze moves across the back of the pews in the direction of our sister. "If the Eastons and the Woods join forces, it could lead to war anyway. And it will be Aurelia who will suffer. This plan might be completely crackers, but it is the only way to ensure her safety and ours."

Kane places his hand on my shoulder in a rare show of affection. "Whatever you need, brother."

I watch him walk back to his seat, a little choked up by his show of solidarity. I'll always have my brothers' backs, and I know they'll always have mine.

It starts to rain, big fat teardrops hammering down on the concrete floor outside the church. It echoes through the arched doorway, creating a soothing backdrop that seems at odds with what is about to happen.

Eventually I hear a vehicle approaching, and I start to straighten from my seat just as I hear the squealing of tyres. I come to my feet at the sound of car doors slamming, and as I do, she appears in the doorway. Her wedding dress is fitted, accentuating her narrow shoulders and prominent collar-bone. She has a veil over her face, hiding her from me. In the shit light of the chapel, it's hard to make out her features beneath the lacy material. I watch as the men all drag her towards me. She struggles against them, but she is no match for their size.

As she gets closer, I start to make out her features beneath the veil, and my heart starts to race. Because I fucking recognise her.

She hasn't seen me yet, or even noticed me. She's too busy struggling against my father's guards. I move before I think about what I'm doing. I shove the nearest man back before slamming my fist into the other man's face. They are both wearing ski masks, so I can't see who they are, but I don't give a fuck. My only focus is on the woman standing in front of me in the bridal gown.

She wraps her arms around her middle, as if she can protect herself from what's happening. Then her eyes come to mine. I watch them flare wide, the fake lashes she's wearing making her irises pop. Everything fades into the background, including the sound of my mother yelling at me. All I'm focused on is my bride.

I step into her space, my chest heaving up and down, then I slowly lift the veil over her head. Her lips are red, the colour of blood, and parted slightly as her own breath tears out of her. She doesn't look anything like the girl I met in the club, the source of all my dreams since that first night we were together, but it is her. I'm certain of it.

"Alice...."

No, not Alice. Sariah fucking Easton, the daughter of a

man we've just made enemies with. The woman I'm supposed to marry.

Her eyes crawl over my face, taking in every inch of me. I can see the shock etched into every line furrowing her brow. She is as surprised as I am. I knew she had secrets. I could see them in her eyes every time we met. I didn't think her secrets were this big. How the hell did she keep hidden who her father is?

"Luke?"

"You two know each other?"

I ignore my mother's question and instead cup Alice's—no, Sariah's— face. The fear in her eyes is still there, but it is muted. "Why am I here?" she asks. "And who are you?"

I want to answer her questions, but once I do, things will change between us. For the moment, I just want to taste her, to feel her. I dip my head and I claim her mouth. She's exactly as I remember—better, even. The kiss is hot, heavy, and despite having an audience, I disappear into her touch. She is all that matters in this instant. If we were alone, I would have pushed her back onto one of the pews, lifted her skirt, and taken her.

When we break apart, she's breathing heavily. "Luke?" There is so much uncertainty in that one word. I brush her hair back, wishing I could see her properly without all that shit on her face. She's made up like a fucking doll and I hate it.

"Sariah. Sariah Easton?"

She glances around the chapel, sees all the unfriendly faces, and doesn't answer. I lift Sariah's face towards me and she gives me her eyes. Fuck, I could get lost in them for days. "No one is going to hurt you, I give you my word." I will destroy anyone who touches her.

"Yes," she admits to her name softly.

"Time is ticking, Lucas," Charlotte says from behind me. I

wish Sariah and I were alone. The last thing I want is a fucking audience right now. "We need to get the wedding underway before the Eastons retaliate."

Sariah looks at me, confusion a clear mask she's wearing. "Wedding?"

"Well, you are dressed for the occasion, darling," Charlotte says in a snippy tone that pisses me off.

I pull Sariah to the side and away from my family as much as I can. I need at least the illusion of privacy, even if there is none in reality. "Do you want to marry Jeremiah Wood?"

Her brows draw together. "Of course not. My father arranged it. I had no choice."

I take her hands in mine, feeling how cold she is. I start to rub her skin, trying to get some heat back into her limbs. "There has to be a wedding, Sariah. Either you to him," I pause, not sure how to address this but figuring it's better to just say the words, "or you to me." Knowing Jeremiah, I understand why she wanted to lose her virginity before marrying him. He would have wrecked her.

She stares at me as if I've lost my mind. Perhaps I have. But all the fears I had about marrying a stranger are no longer there, because marrying Sariah, Alice, whatever the fuck her name is, is no longer an overwhelming prospect. It feels right, like this was meant to be. I was supposed to meet her that night in the club, and she is supposed to be standing in front of me in a wedding dress, ready to say our vows.

"You want to marry me? We hardly know each other, Luke."

I shake my head. "We'll learn about each other." I can't stop from kissing her again, needing to reassure her that this is meant to be. "You have to make this decision, and you have to do it now. We are running out of time."

"You brought me here to marry you? You didn't know

who I was. You didn't know if I'd want to marry you." Anger laces her tone.

"We can put you back in the car and take you to the church where Jeremiah is waiting, if you prefer," Anthony says.

I ignore my father's words and focus solely on Sariah. "Little dove, there's going to be a wedding today. There's no avoiding that. It is the only way I can keep my family safe. I know it feels like all your choices are being taken from you, and I'm sorry for that, but I was set to marry whoever walked through that door. I'm so fucking relieved it was you."

"Jeremiah and my father will kill me if I do not go ahead with the wedding he's planned."

"If you are my wife, I will protect you from any danger. I promise you that."

She peers up at me as if I could be her saviour. I want desperately to fill that role for her. "You can't protect me from their wrath. No one can save me from that." Her voice is small as she says this, and I hate that it is. No one will ever make her feel small again.

"If they come for you, they will have to deal with the weight of the Fraser Empire. And I can assure you, Sariah, our reach is long. If you are my wife, I can keep you safe. Let me protect you, little dove." I squeeze her hands.

"This is crazy. We've only met each other a few times."

I run my knuckles down her cheek, and she leans into my touch, which I take as a win. "That is true, but you can't deny there is chemistry between us. You like me as much as I like you."

"I do like you, I can't lie about that, but that doesn't mean we should rush into this. Maybe we should just take a moment and think…"

I take her hands again in mine. "If I had it, I would give you all the time you need in the world to process this. But this is about to cause a war. We have to act now. What do you say? Do you want to be my wife?"

"Declan is going to be furious."

"He loves you. You're his daughter. He'll come around when he realises that this is a done deal. That will bring the Eastons into our alliance."

She shakes her head. "I doubt he'd care if I lived or died. My only use to him was as a bargaining chip."

I search Sariah's face, wondering if she is telling the truth. I don't see any lie in her eyes. "What do you mean?"

She doesn't answer. She closes her eyes for a moment as if trying to calibrate herself. I wonder what the fuck is running through her head, because mine is rolling with thoughts. We shouldn't be doing this so fast, she's right about that, but I know Wood is going to be furious at losing his bride, and he's going to take that out on the only person he can. Sariah. To protect her I need her in my circle. When she opens her eyes again, I see the resolve shining back at me. "Tell me your name."

"Lucas Fraser."

Her eyes dart around as she looks at my siblings and parents, as if she is trying to put names to faces. "I've traded one fire for another. Either way I get burnt." She huffs out a breath and steels her shoulders. "This is completely insane, but yes, I'll marry you."

CHAPTER 16

Sariah

I've traded one insanity for another. In the weeks leading up to the wedding, I prayed to every god I could think of for Luke to save me. Now he's offering an olive branch, a life raft to a drowning woman, and I hesitate to take it. This is exactly what I wanted. Luke and me, together. But this isn't just riding off into the sunset and seeing where things go. This is a commitment, one that can't be undone once it's made.

That scares me.

But what is the alternative? Marry Jeremiah and do what Declan demanded of me? Or have an opportunity to choose my own path? At least I like Luke. There are feelings there, for sure. When he touches me, I ignite. When Jeremiah laid his hands on me, I felt sick. But marriage is such a big step. Knowing he's a Fraser changes everything. The Fraser family has a reputation that even I'm aware of. Declan sheltered me from a lot, but he couldn't keep me in the dark from everything. I heard things growing up, so I know about the families who rule the London criminal underbelly. I know Declan was scared of them.

Of their reach.

Of the things they were rumoured to have done.

If I'd have known who Luke was when I met him, I would have run the other way. I don't even want to think about what he would have done to me if he knew my true identity.

Luke leads me over to the front of the church and takes my hands in his. "This has to be quick."

There is a hint of apology in his voice, as if he wishes he could give me better.

"We could wait and get to know each other better."

"If you remain unmarried, there is a risk your father will get you back and hand you over to Wood. Are you willing to take that chance?"

No, I'm not. The last thing I want is that man near me. I have no doubt my father would drag me back and force me in front of that altar to marry the Butcher of Manchester. If he survived his shooting, anyway. The last I saw he was bleeding heavily from the shoulder.

I peer up into Luke's eyes. "Let's do this."

He glances over my head towards the older blonde lady. "We're ready."

Luke keeps his eyes locked on me throughout the ceremony. The priest seems nervous as he says the words of the ceremony. I can't even believe I'm doing this. It seems like a surreal dream, but part of it also seems right. Luke is correct when he says this is the only way to protect me. I can't be married again once already wed. Whatever plans Declan will have for me, at least he can't sell me to a man twice my age.

I have to hope Luke will protect me from the worst of Declan's wrath.

Luke slips a wedding ring onto my finger. It's too big, but it's beautiful, rose gold inlaid with diamonds. It makes me wonder how long they've been planning to snatch me for. They are prepared.

The priest gets to the "I do" part, and Luke gives his agreement easily.

The words feel foreign as I say them myself. "I do."

"You may now kiss the bride." The priest steps back, closing his Bible.

Luke's eyes are hungry as he takes me in. I've never been wanted before I met him, and I like how it makes me feel. "Hello, Mrs Fraser."

Sariah Fraser.

It doesn't feel as odd as I expect. He dips his head and takes my mouth. The kiss is tender and filled with warmth that heats my whole body. His hand snakes around my waist, pulling me closer as his fingers tighten against my hips. My pulse thunders in my chest as his masculine scent envelops me. This is so unlike all the other kisses we've shared. There is so much promise in it. It steals my breath and leaves me gasping for air when he finally releases my lips.

The blonde lady hands me a pen. "Sign here." She points to a dotted line on a document laid out on the altar behind the priest.

I glance at Luke, not sure what it is I'm signing.

"It's the wedding register," he explains. "We both have to sign it to make the wedding legal."

I don't hesitate. I take the pen she offers and I sign my name. Luke takes the pen from me, his eyes filled with so much warmth. He signs too before taking my hands back in his as the blonde lady and the older man also sign. I can tell he is bursting to talk to me and I can't wait to be alone with him.

"Time to get gone," the blonde lady says as she puts the pen down. She scares me. She has a look in her eye that tells me she's constantly planning. "Easton won't wait long before retaliating. Let him know that his daughter is safely married into a family now."

"He's not going to take this lying down," I say. "Declan doesn't like anyone playing the game but him."

The blonde woman waves this off. "You are his child. There's nothing a parent will not do for their own."

If they are banking on that, they are barking up the wrong tree. Declan despises me. It sits on the tip of my tongue to tell them the truth, that I'm not really Declan's daughter, but something stops me. Secrets are best kept close to the chest. Once they are out, there is no putting them back in the box.

"Don't worry about Declan Easton," Luke says. "My family will handle him—and Jeremiah Wood."

He leads me outside the chapel, refusing to release his hold on my hand the whole time. Considering I barely know him, it shouldn't make butterflies flutter inside my stomach, but it does. Luke has a way of getting under my skin far too easily.

The rain is hammering down and bouncing off the pavement, so we run to the car waiting outside the church. I was bundled into the back of one when I was brought here; I didn't expect to be leaving under my own steam in another. This whole thing feels bizarre. Like I'm living somebody else's life or I'm seeing everything play like a movie reel. I just married a man I've only had sex with three times. What was I thinking?

That he could offer an escape.

That he could be the lesser of two evils.

And that he might give me protection when Declan comes calling.

As we get into the back of the car, his bodyguard, Winters, gets into the front seat. Now I understand why Luke needs one. He is a mob boss's son.

Luke helps me with the enormous skirt of my dress, pushing it down out of the way.

"I hope you know what you are doing. You just unleashed

a war on your family. Declan will never let this go. He doesn't like to be humiliated."

"You call him Declan. Not Father or Dad."

It's hard to call someone who beats you a parent. The make-up covers most of the bruising on my face and neck. It's why I'm so made up, but the wedding planner couldn't hide the worst of it. My body is littered with purple and black marks, and my ribs still hurt, something the dress is not helping with as it's so heavy. "I don't view him as my father."

Because he's not. I don't say this out loud because while on some level I trust Luke, I'm not sure what he would do with the information. I'm not ready to give this part of myself up to him yet.

"I know that feeling."

"You don't get on with yours?"

"My father likes to control my life, as does my mother, and neither sits right with me. I hate feeling like a chess piece to be moved around on the board."

I know precisely how he feels because it's how I feel too. I'm just part of Declan's games. "But they love you?"

He makes a noise in the back of his throat that is somewhere between a laugh and a snort. "I don't think either of my parents are capable of love. They see me as a resource that they can use to further their agenda."

"We have that in common." The car starts to move and I peer out of the side window. "Where are we going?"

"Back to my apartment. I need to put you somewhere safe."

There will be nowhere safe for me to hide. Nor for his family. "What is the endgame here?" I ask.

"To stop your father and Jeremiah Wood from creating an alliance. If we can bring the Easton syndicate onside, all the better, but that wasn't the goal. My mother was terrified of the strength your father might have if he combined forces with Manchester syndicates. We had to stop it, no matter the cost."

I watch the London skyline whizz past the window, my mind feeling full. I have no idea what I'm supposed to do. I've never been in this kind of situation before, and my upbringing certainly hasn't prepared me for being stuck in the middle of a battle between three syndicate factions. "You really would have married whoever came through that door?"

"I would have done what my family needed me to do."

"Even though I am a stranger."

"Were you not set to marry a stranger yourself?"

"Not of my own free will, Luke. You were waiting willingly for your bride to walk through those doors. How do you do that? How do you just... turn off that part of your brain that says this is wrong?"

He considers my question for a moment before he speaks. "My whole life I have been trained for one thing. To take care of my family. To protect my sister. I'll do that by whatever means necessary, even if it means marrying somebody I've never met before."

He cups my face, and I can't help but leaning into his touch. I've missed him. Missed what we had, even as short lived as it was. It is the first time in my life since my mother died that I felt wanted, needed, desired. I'll admit I got caught up in the drama of it all. In the hype and the emotions. I think I still am, considering I married Luke in a legally binding ceremony.

"Did you never want to just deviate? Do your own thing?"

He rubs his thumb over the apple of my cheek. "Did you? Why did you stay so obedient?"

Because I'm terrified of Declan. I feared being out in the world more than I feared him. The world is a dangerous place for a mob princess, and it was always a case of better the devil you know.

"I didn't have a choice," I say quietly. "Declan ruled my life, every inch of it, from what I wear to who I marry. He owned me."

Anger clouds his eyes for a moment. "No one owns you, Sariah."

I cock my eyebrow at him, not sure how to take his outburst. "Not even you?"

"I'm your husband, not your keeper." He spits the words out, and I resist the urge to recoil from his ire. He notices my reaction and his brow draws together. "You don't need to be scared of me. I'll not hurt you. I promise you that."

He says this, but I don't really know him well enough to know what he would or would not do, and I've been hurt by people I was meant to trust before. It isn't easy for me to put my faith in someone else.

"I hope that's a promise you can keep," I say to the man who is now my husband.

Husband.

The word still seems foreign to me. I have a husband. I rub a hand over my forehead, feeling my temple starting to throb. "I can't believe we got married."

He pulls me closer, holding my chin between his fingers as he presses his mouth to mine. I want to argue, to tell him this isn't the time or the place. We have too much to discuss, but I lean into his touch, my tongue sweeping over his. As always, my belly tingles the moment his hands are on me. Luke cares about me, and not because of what I can bring to the table, because he didn't know who I was in the beginning. He was kind to me at a time in my life when that was a rare occurrence. He treated me like a human being, not a chip to be bartered. He pulled me out of the darkness when I was drowning, and he gave me the best gift he could have given me. He gave me a choice. No one has ever done that for me.

His hand slips around the back of my neck and tightens. When his eyes meet mine, I see the fire in them, the heat. "Get used to being my wife, little dove, because you are now a Fraser."

That should scare me, but it doesn't.

Before today the Frasers weren't our enemy, but stealing me and shooting Declan the way they did means they've moved into that territory. I should side with the man who has raised me all these years, but I don't want to.

I don't owe Declan my allegiance or my support. I don't owe it to Luke either, but I'm more inclined to give it to him. He's never done anything to hurt me, and I don't think he would. We're both completely besotted with each other, and I like the intensity of that feeling, even though I'm sure it won't last. Good things never do in my life.

For now, all I can do is ride this wave. Because Luke makes me feel alive in a way I never have. It's that strength of feeling for him that scares me the most. I've never relied on anyone before, but I think I already lean on him.

I want to get to know him better. It's all I wanted the whole time I was with him. In the club there wasn't time to really talk in depth. We were driven more by our needs, by our desire to be together. Things are different now. This isn't just about sex or a connection. Marriage is different. It's not about immediate gratification, but long-term happiness. Do I get to be happy? I've never considered what a life like that would look like. I just accepted my lot and resigned myself to a life of hell and misery.

Luke gives me hope. Yes, he is the son of a crime boss, and I'm sure his slate is not clean, but he's the first person in my life who doesn't seem to want to control me or make me dance to their tune. He doesn't want me to be the pretty doll on the shelf. That makes me fall for him a little more.

It's more than that though. Declan told me no one would ever want me, but I'm starting to realise my father talked a lot of crap. I feel special with Luke, like I am worthy of his attention. It's been a long time since anybody gave me that. So long I barely remember what it's like to be loved or cared for. I'm addicted to the feelings he brings to the forefront when we are together. The natural high I get from being around him can't be simulated. I've never wanted a person in my life as much as I want him. I crave meaning something to someone.

"What happens when my father realises you've taken me?" I ask in a hesitant voice. Asking questions usually gets me new bruises, so I can't stop from bracing myself. But the hit never comes. Luke just squeezes my hand.

"Your father will either come to our side or he will side with Jeremiah Wood. We hope he will do the former, but if he does the latter, we will destroy him." He says this so easily, as if talking about the weather rather than murdering people. I know this darkness exists in men. I've seen it in Declan many times, but for some reason, Luke's words chill me to the bone.

"I don't want anyone to get hurt because of me." The thought of Luke getting injured makes my gut churn.

"Not for you to worry about, little dove," he says, his tone a little stern.

I shouldn't let it rile me, but it does. I'm tired of being told what I should feel and what I should think. I'm tired of being told how I should react. Now that I've tasted freedom, been given a hint of it, I'm loath to give it back.

"It concerns me, Luke, so it is for me to worry about. I can't just switch it off and pretend life is okay even though you may be risking your neck to keep me safe."

"Little dove, you married a Fraser. We take care of our own and protect family to the death. I will keep you safe and be sensible doing it, I promise."

Neither of us speaks until the car stops outside a large

126

building. It must have at least thirty floors, maybe—it's hard to tell from my vantage point. My heart starts to race. Once again, I'm in a situation where I have no idea what the outcome will be, only this time I'm not afraid. I'm interested to see what the future holds for me as Mrs Sariah Fraser.

CHAPTER 17

Lucas

The relief I felt when I pulled back that veil and realised it was Alice—Sariah Easton—standing in front of me and not a stranger is still with me as we walk into the building. I can only imagine how we look. I'm in a suit and Sariah is wearing a wedding dress. We look like we just fled the church, which is kind of what we did do. The urge to get her home and safe before the shit hits the fan is overwhelming. I want to protect her. No, I *need* to protect her. She is still keeping secrets, and I plan on getting to the bottom of all of them. As her husband, I want to know everything about her.

She gazes everywhere as we step into the foyer past the doorman, who gives me a jut of his chin in recognition. The suite once belonged to my brother, Zeke, but when he married Bailey, they moved into her family home so they didn't have to uproot the kids. I'm not complaining. I gained a swish penthouse apartment out of it.

I go into the lift, pulling Sariah with me. She comes without question, something I'm going to have to tear out of her. I get the impression she's used to being the obedient servant. I don't want that. I don't want a sheep. I want someone with their own thoughts and feelings. Whatever trauma she's been through has ground her down in a way I can't even fathom.

Winters gets into the lift behind us, and I find myself smirking. Last time the three of us were in a lift together, I fingered Sariah's pretty pussy. If she wasn't wearing so many layers of lace, I'd hoist her skirts up and take her now. Instead, I settle for holding her hand and rubbing my thumb over the back of it. I can feel her trembling. I want to dismantle all her demons and fix everything, but that will take time. Luckily, we have plenty of it because I take the "until death us do part" bit of our vows seriously.

When the lift doors open on the floor, Winters moves to make sure it's safe. We step off the lift and wait for him to return. When he does, I dismiss him. I wait until the elevator doors slide shut on him before I turn back to Sariah. I want to take her now, push inside her and fuck her until she's screaming my name, but her wide frightened eyes still my hand. "I meant it when I said you had nothing to fear from me."

"I'm not scared of you," she admits. She might be the only person on the planet who isn't. "I'm scared of what comes next."

I rake my fingers through my hair. "Nothing to be scared of there either. I like my women willing, Sariah. I want you to enjoy what we do as much as I do."

She shakes her head. "Not scared of... sex with you. We've done that before."

"Then what is bothering you?"

"That I don't know the first thing about you." She raises her arms out at her sides and gestures around to the grandeur of the penthouse apartment. It is lavish, obnoxiously so, but it's all Zeke's doing. He left everything behind when he

129

moved, other than his belongings. He picked all the furniture and the decor. I would not have chosen such an ostentatious design.

"What would you like to know?"

"The woman in the chapel—she called you Lucas. Do you prefer that to Luke?"

I cock my brow at her question. "Do you really care what I'm called?"

"Yes, of course I care. I don't want to call you a name you don't like."

I walk over to the table in the middle of the room and grab a bottle of scotch from the cupboard underneath. "Do you want one?" I expect her to say no, but she surprises me by nodding. I pull out two glasses and begin to pour. "The blonde woman is my mother, Charlotte. She is one of the few people who calls me Lucas. Most of the time, my friends and my siblings call me Luke. That is why I gave you that name. Because it is the one I identify with more." I pass her the glass, and she takes it with two hands. She downs the alcohol in one hit. "Thirsty?" I smirk.

"I don't usually drink very much, but today seems a good day to indulge. Why did you pick me?"

She moves around to the edge of the sofa and manages to sit down in a plume of skirts and lace. I sit on the seat opposite her, wanting to look at her face as I talk to her. "Charlotte manoeuvred the wedding. She wanted to break the treaty your father had with Jeremiah."

"Why? What does it matter who I marry?"

"Peace exists in London because things are carefully balanced. Marrying you to the head of the Manchester syndicate would have upset that balance. Your father is seeking allies from further afield, men he can call in when needed. That concerned us. If your father had the weight of Manchester behind him as well, he could have unseated the other London syndicates. We had to act. Stopping your marriage, stopping the alliance, was imperative. Charlotte tried to offer a deal, but your father wouldn't hear it. He was determined to go ahead with the wedding, and we could never allow it to happen. We couldn't exactly crash the church. It would have been too dangerous. Two crime families plus whoever else was on the guest list.... It would have been a bloodbath. That's why we took you on the road. Your father didn't have much security around you, so you were easy pickings."

She places her hands in her lap and peers down at them as she takes all this information in. "You could have killed me. That would have stopped the wedding and any future alliance. Why did you agree to the marriage instead?"

"Because you're an innocent, Sariah. You didn't deserve to die for your father's crimes. Besides, this way there is a chance your father may come around and support us. That would send Jeremiah back to his rathole and restore peace to the city."

Her eyes come up to meet mine, and I see the heaviness weighing on her shoulders. "Jeremiah will never return to Manchester. He will see this as a slight. He thought he owned me, that I was his toy to do with as he wanted. You've taken that from him. He will come at your family hard, and he will not stop until he has what he wants. Me."

"He can try, but he won't find the Frasers an easy target. If he has any common sense, he will walk away and let this go."

She gives me a sad smile. "If you were in his position, would you just walk away?"

I wouldn't. It must show my face because she says, "Exactly."

I go over to Sariah and sit next to her, needing to be in her space. "Wood.... He is why you were so desperate to lose your virginity?"

Sariah bobs her head up and down. "It's stupid, but I wanted my first time to be on my terms. He made it clear he wasn't going to be gentle, and I was scared. I mean, I couldn't guarantee it would be gentle with a stranger either, but Jeremiah aimed to hurt me. I saw it in his eyes when I met him. I figured if I'd at least had sex before I went to his bed, it would be less... painful."

"I hope I made your first time bearable."

She snaps her eyes up to me and I see this shock register in her face. "Bearable? It was more than that. It was the best night of my life, Luke. You made me feel things I'd never felt. You made me feel wanted. Needed. And I wasn't scared. Stupid, isn't it, considering the fact that you were a complete stranger to me. You made me feel safe. I can never thank you enough for that."

I don't want to talk about Jeremiah Wood any longer. The man makes me want to commit homicide. I'm glad I was her first. And not just because the primal man inside me loves knowing I'm the only person who's been inside her, but also because she deserves better than what Jeremiah Wood would give her. I'm not even sure I delivered what she was worthy of. I brush a loose curl back from her face. "I missed you."

She seems surprised by my admission, but it is the truth. I felt like we were starting to build something together, something special. I want to pick up where we left off, but I want her to be in this with me too. I don't wait for permission. I push her back onto the sofa and come down on top of her. I claim her mouth instantly, sweeping my tongue along the seam of her lips until she grants me access inside. There's no hesitation from her. She wants this too. I kiss her like she's my oxygen and I need her to breathe. There's a desperation in my movements and need to have her. My body remembers everything we did together and how good it felt. I want that again.

I want her.

I know what we have is infatuation right now, but there are sparks of something else, as well as mutual respect, that could turn into more. I never expected to care for the woman I was forced to marry, but I do care about Sariah. I find I want to please her, and that's something I've never felt when I've been with other women. I have a wealth of experience, but not of relationships. I'm usually a fuck and leave them kind of guy. I'm twenty-two, and I didn't think I was ready to settle down, but with her the thought doesn't scare me as much as it should.

I wrap my fingers around her throat in a loose hold, but the moment I touch her, she moans. That makes my dick go solid in my trousers. She is a wet dream.

Kissing her isn't enough. I need to be inside her. I need to feel our connection after being separated. "The dress.... It needs to come off."

I help her sit up and then pull her to her feet, noting how heated her eyes are. She wants this too, and that spurs me on. Getting her out of the contraption is not an easy task. The dress is complicated, and it takes some manoeuvring to take it off. Eventually I manage to get her out of the skirts so she's standing there in white lace underwear. She has stockings on and a tiny pair of white knickers. She's not wearing a bra, so her tits are on display.

I should take the moment to just admire her figure, but my eyes are drawn to the litany of bruises that cover her chest and legs. They are a greenish brown colour, indicating they are a little old and are healing, but this was done recently.

"What the fuck happened to you?" I demand through gritted teeth. She shrinks back and I have to force myself to be calm. I don't want to frighten her, but right now red is filming my vision. She was beaten. I can tell by the catalogue of injuries she's carrying. The worst of it is around her left rib cage. Those bruises are still black.

"Declan doesn't like it when I do things that go against him," she admits in a soft voice.

"Your own father did this to you?" I had always assumed Declan kept her hidden because he loved her in the same way we love Aurelia, but no one could inflict this kind of damage and claim to love the person.

I see the shame in her eyes, and I hate that she thinks it's hers to carry. We don't beat women. We don't have much of a moral code, but there are some lines we will not cross. This is one of them. I imagine somebody doing this to my sister and my anger roars through my veins. "If I'd known—"

"You wouldn't have done anything," she says. "Women in our world are seen but not heard. No one would have cared."

But she's wrong. I care. The strength of the fury racing through me takes me by surprise. I've only ever given a shit about my sister, but I find myself willing to throw down to protect and avenge the wrongs done to Sariah.

She tries to cover herself, embarrassed maybe, but I pull her hands away. "Don't hide yourself from me." Even covered in bruises, Sariah is beautiful, and the thought of her with that crusty old bastard makes my stomach twist.

"I want to fuck you, but I don't want to hurt you."

She peers up at me through her fake eyelashes that make her eyes look bigger and more pronounced. "You won't."

She is lying, to herself and to me. But I can't resist her. She calls to me like a fucking siren.

I reach out a hand and cup her breast. It's soft beneath my touch and as I roll her nipple between my fingers, she hisses out a breath between her teeth.

"Luke...."

I silence Sariah by stepping up to her and wrapping my arms around her waist. Pulling her closer against me, I grind my cock against that tiny scrap of lace that covers her pussy. She reacts as if she's never been touched before, with more pants erupting from her mouth as she closes her eyes, taking in all the sensations as I press harder against her cunt. I've barely touched her and already she sounds like she's coming undone. "Luke."

Hearing my name on her tongue unravels me in a way I've never experienced. I feel half-crazed with desire. I need more from her.

"Help me undress," I order.

She obliges, her fingers fumbling to push my suit jacket off my shoulders. It takes her what feels like forever to undo the buttons of my shirt, but finally she shoves that off my body too. This is nothing like the other times we've been together. She seems more nervous, which surprises me. It's not like we don't know each other's bodies.

Impatient, I do the rest. Getting out of my trousers and shoes takes me less than a minute, and then I stand just in my boxers in front of her.

She surprises me by reaching out and palming my cock through my boxers. I suck in a breath through my teeth, my balls tightening. I can't take this anymore. I need to be inside her.

I grab her and hoist her into my arms. Her legs instinctively wrap around my back, knotting at the ankles as I take her mouth in a heavy kiss. She loops her arms around my neck as I stroke up her back. I want to show her something different than the first few times we fucked, but my need to have her outweighs everything. This is going to be hard, fast, and dirty.

I walk us into the bedroom and drop her onto the mattress, coming down on top of her. She looks like a fucking angel dressed in white. I press a kiss against the bare skin of her thigh above her stocking, close to that apex I want to devour. Her thighs tremble as I get closer to her pussy, and when I kiss the material over her slit, I can feel how wet it is.

"Is this all for me, Sariah?" I ask as I slip my finger under the lace and run a finger through her wetness.

My wife lets out a moan as I slide two digits inside her. "Yes!"

Spurred on by her encouragement, I start to piston my fingers in and out of her as I find her mouth. I kiss her until I can hardly breathe, and then I make my way down the column of her throat to that dip between her collarbones.

She is panting hard now, making little mewls of pleasure that make me fucking happy. I've never cared about a woman's enjoyment before. Their only job was to service me, but from the moment I met Sariah, I wanted to make it good for her. I want to give her things that I've never given anyone before. And not just because she's beautiful, even though she is.

Sariah and I are lost souls, caught up in our families' machinations. I didn't lie when I said I was relieved it was her standing in front of me and not a stranger. I would have done my duty, but I feel better knowing she is mine.

I move down her body, trailing kisses along the length of her torso until I get to her belly. I press a kiss just above her pubic bone before I suck her clit. I keep my fingers moving in tandem with my tongue, driving her wild. She fists the sheets beneath her as if it can ground her, but it can't. When I'm done with her, she's going to be begging my name for release.

She doesn't take long to build to her climax. I feel Sariah quake beneath me, her thighs twitching as her release grows. She twists her head to the side as she yells out my name, making my balls draw tighter. Her pussy still throbbing around my fingers, I pull out of her and push my boxers down my legs. I quickly grab a condom from the bedside table and roll it on. Then I line up my cock with her hole, pushing through her wetness so I can slide into her tight cunt. She grips my forearms as I press into her to the root. Fuck. I drag my bottom lip between my teeth as I try to keep control. This isn't going to last long.

"Please, move," she commands, this time the one giving the orders.

I do as she asks and drag my cock back out of her channel before slamming back inside. We both groan at the sensations that envelop us. My head feels fuzzy, delirious even. I can hardly focus on anything but pumping my hips back and forth. Fucking Sariah has always felt different, but knowing she's my wife while I'm pounding her is a completely new experience. I feel connected to her in a way I've never felt to any other woman. I fucking like it.

I rotate my hips, pushing deeper inside her and hitting that spot that makes her arch her back off the bed.

I hold her hands over her head, pinning her down. She peers up at me with such trust in her eyes that I never want to fucking break it. "Luke...." She says my name as though she's invoking it in fucking prayer. I'm no one's saviour, but I find I want to be that for her.

I glide into her over and over, locking my eyes with hers. I can't tear them away, and I don't want to. I need to see her as she goes over the edge. Sariah pulls her bottom lip between her teeth as if she can silence her screams. Then her body vibrates and her pussy clenches and pulses, squeezing my dick. My balls draw up, and I let out a garbled sound as I spill inside her.

Breathing hard, I try not to collapse on top of her, even though that's what I want to do. My legs feel like jelly, my whole body trembling in the aftermath of my orgasm.

I pull out of her and lie next to her, tugging her onto my chest. I kiss her forehead and she nuzzles against me. No matter what happens, I will keep my wife safe from those who mean to harm her, including her own father. No one will ever lay hands on Sariah in anger again. Part of me hopes that her father stands against us, because I have an overwhelming urge to put a bullet in that cunt.

Sariah Fraser is now my wife and I'll do anything to protect her.

CHAPTER 18

Sariah

I wake with Luke wrapped around me. His leg is thrown over mine as he hugs me from behind, and his nose is nuzzled into the back of my neck. For a moment I lie still, just taking in the fact that he is now my husband.

I had dreams of this. Wanted it desperately to be true, and now that it is, I'm not sure what to do.

I stroke my fingers over his arm that is thrown over my waist. The feeling of his skin against mine leaves me feeling warm and sated. I enjoy the moment because I know this cannot last. Despite what Luke thinks, Declan is not going to roll over and play nicely.

"You're awake." The sleepy voice from behind me makes my lips pull into a smile. He burrows his nose deeper into my neck, and I tilt my head to give him better access.

"Morning."

"How are you feeling?"

"I feel good." I feel better than good. In between my legs aches in a delicious way. He hadn't been rough last night, but he certainly left a lasting impression.

"We need to get you on birth control. Next time I'm inside you, I want to feel you."

"Birth control?" I peer up at him.

"Does that worry you, little dove?"

"A bit." Better than the alternative though. I'm not ready to be pregnant. I'm barely wrapping my head around the fact that I'm married.

His hand goes to my belly, splaying over where a child would grow. "I don't want any unplanned mishaps. Not yet."

I nod because I agree with him. We're young and our lives are unpredictable. We lie clinched together for a while with him spooning my back. Eventually he turns me around so I'm facing him, our noses inches from each other's. His eyes roam over my face as if he's committing every inch of it to his memory. "Yesterday was a bit wild."

My brow rises. "A bit?"

He plays with my nipple, making it hard for me to concentrate on what he says next. "Okay, it was out-of-this-world insane. Do you regret it?"

I shake my head before sucking in a breath as he rolls my nipple between his fingers. "Luke," I say on a rush of air, taking a moment to reclaim my equilibrium. "No, I don't regret anything."

My thoughts scatter as he closes the gap between us, slanting his head so he can claim my mouth. The kiss is tender, something I wouldn't expect from a man like him. I get lost in the sensations that are surrounding me. As he pushes his semihard cock against my exposed pussy, I let out a whimper.

"I want to fuck my wife."

Wife.

That's going to take some getting used to, although the title feels like it fits already. I reach between us and take his cock in my hand. His eyes never leave my face as I move my hand over his shaft, bolder than I feel.

"Little dove, are you trying to drive me crazy?"

I don't answer him. I just keep working over his dick. I enjoy being able to pleasure him. I want to make him feel as good as he makes me feel. I have no idea if what I'm doing is right, but when he closes his eyes and tucks his bottom lip between his teeth, I figure I'm on the right track.

He is getting harder in my hand and his breath is coming out quicker now. He reaches down, to wrap his fingers around my wrist, stopping me. "You keep that up and I'm going to come in your hand."

I smile as he rolls over and opens the drawer at the side of the bed. He pulls out a condom and rolls it on.

He comes back to lie in front of me and tucks my hair behind my ears as his cock nudges against my centre. He keeps his eyes locked on me as he slowly pushes inside my body. My pussy stretches to accommodate him, a delicious ache that makes my breath rip out of me in a happy sounding pant.

After we make love, we both shower and get changed. He lends me some of his clothes–a pair of jogging bottoms and a T-shirt that is baggy on me. When I emerge from the bedroom after making myself look presentable, I find him sitting in the kitchen area of the extensive penthouse suite at the breakfast bar. My eyes are drawn to the floor-to-ceiling windows that look out over the London landscape. It's an amazing view.

"Come and have breakfast with me," Luke says.

I turn back to the room, pulling my gaze from the view. The decor is masculine, different shades of grey, white, and black, the furniture square and blocky. There are no feminine touches whatsoever, though it does feel lived in. There is clutter in the kitchen area that suggests it's not just for show.

I go to him and slip onto the stool next to him. His hand slides over my back, a possessive move that makes my stomach flip. He always wants to be touching me. I like that.

"What do you want to eat?"

"What are the choices?"

He reels off a list of things that sound delicious, and I realise I haven't eaten since the day before the wedding. I felt too sick to eat on the day itself, and Luke and I spent most of the night in bed together. Food was the last thing on my mind. Now that he's brought up eating, I'm suddenly ravenous.

"Eggs and toast sounds great," I say. I don't know why, but I feel a little shy around him. This is a man who has seen me naked, has touched my most intimate parts, and yet being fully clothed standing in his kitchen feels strange. He doesn't let on that he feels the same. He pushes up off the stool and goes to the fridge. I watch the muscles ripple beneath his tee, my mouth suddenly dry. "If you married me for my culinary skills, you're going to be very disappointed," I joke. "We had people who did that for us."

He doesn't laugh, but his lips quirk at the corners. "I don't expect you to be at home all day like some beacon of domesticity. I want you to find your own path, Sariah. Indulge in things that you enjoy and that keep you happy. I meant what I said. I'm not your keeper, and your life is yours to live as you see fit. As long as you don't take risks with your safety, and of course you have to have security wherever you go, but other than that, you are free."

His words make a lump settle in my throat, one that feels like it's choking me, cutting my air supply off. I've never had a moment of freedom since I was born. My life has always been what other people dictated.

I go to the coffee machine, giving him my back as my eyes fill with tears. I never expected to have freedom in my marriage. I know for a fact Jeremiah would have controlled me as much as my father did, maybe even more. The fact that Luke wants to give me autonomy over my own self makes the depth of feeling I have for him intensify.

"Do you want a top up?" I ask, swallowing down my emotions. I don't look at him. I can't. If I do I'll cry, and I don't want to be weak in front of him.

I hear him move behind me and feel his presence at my back as his hands go to my shoulders. He moulds his body against my spine, lifting my hair off my neck so he can kiss the dip between my shoulders. It feels amazing. And I wish we could get lost like this and not have to face reality.

But sooner or later, our lives are going to come knocking.

My father and Jeremiah are going to want to make the Frasers suffer for the humiliation they have caused. I push that out of my head as my breath starts to quicken. I swear Luke has a direct line to my pussy. Every touch leaves me panting. I grip the edge of the counter in front of me as his hand slips around my front under my T-shirt and cups my breast. I dip my head as I make a garbled sound that doesn't sound human.

He kisses down my neck before he releases me and moves back to the stove. It seems as if he doesn't want to let me go, and that makes happiness swell in my chest. I manage to grab my coffee mug and I top his cup up, even though he never said what he wanted. I don't know how to be a wife, but I want to learn. I want to do things that please Luke and make our marriage happy.

I turn back to him, leaning my hip against the counter as I cradle my mug between my hands. The coffee smells divine and expensive. It infuses my nose.

"You're going to need a whole new wardrobe. I'll have someone fetch whatever you want. Just make a list of what you need."

"Okay."

"When the doc comes to talk to you about birth control, I'll have her take a look at your injuries."

I stiffen at his words. I don't want anyone to see my

143

shame. I don't want to feel the humiliation of other people knowing what I've suffered. It's bad enough Luke has seen it. "I'm fine. The bruises are mostly healed, and I'm not in pain."

He twists to look at me. "Your body is covered in marks. I could tell there was a couple of times you were uncomfortable last night. If nothing else, the doctor will be able to give you painkillers."

The fact that he cares melts my insides. "Honestly, Luke, I'm okay. I don't need to see anyone. The injuries are over a week old."

He doesn't look assured. "I wasn't asking, little dove."

I puff out a breath at his bossiness. "Okay. Fine. If it puts your mind at ease."

He breaks an egg into the pan, which sizzles, then he finishes making breakfast and carries both our plates to the breakfast bar. I slide onto the stool and start tucking into my meal, my stomach growling. I've barely taken four mouthfuls when Luke's phone starts to ring.

He mutters a curse under his breath before he answers the call. I continue to eat while I half listen to the one-sided conversation. I only tune in when I hear my father's name. "It was Declan?"

I place my fork on the edge of my plate, my stomach suddenly twisting, and I give Luke my full attention as he continues to talk. "I did try to warn Charlotte this would happen. She wouldn't fucking listen." There's a pause as he listens to the voice on the other end of the line. "My only concern is keeping everyone safe. Do you want to bring Aurelia here? She and Sariah will be safe at the penthouse."

A pang of jealousy hits me in the gut, completely unfounded and out of the blue. Who's Aurelia?

"I need to wait with Sariah until the doctor comes and then I'm all yours." Guilt washes over me as I realise I'm holding him back from doing what he needs to do with his family. "She's fine. It's just routine." I wait until he gets off the phone, and as soon as he hangs up, he spits out a "Fuck!"

"If you need to leave, you should go."

"Not going anywhere yet, but my family does need me."

"My father knows it was your family who took me." It's not a question because I already know the answer. My stomach feels like it's filling with ice, and the same cold feeling spreads through my veins.

"He was always going to find out. Charlotte needed him to be involved in the negotiations. That isn't the problem."

Negotiations.

A bargain.

That's all I'll ever be. I may have convinced myself that Luke wants me because he's interested in me, but in reality I am a business transaction. I step away from him, feeling my heart tighten. I was so swept up in the dream, in the relief of escaping Jeremiah Wood, that I didn't consider whether Luke is just playing a role.

Luke's eyes narrow as he watches me distance myself from him. "Sariah?"

"I don't expect you to love me, Luke. I know I was just a means to an end, but it's hard when you refer to things as negotiations." I can't keep the sadness from my voice as I say these words. I had prayed so hard for the fairy-tale ending, but I'd forgotten I don't exist in a world where happy endings occur. My own mother was murdered by my father. I know the realities of being a mob princess.

"You're my wife. Mine. Do you understand me? This is a real marriage for me, and I hope it is for you as well." He takes my chin in his hand. "I did this for my family. I can't lie about that, but I want you."

His words ease some of the tension in my shoulders and across my back. "It's real for me too, but you're going to resent me in time. I'm going to bring a whirlwind of trouble to your door. Because I know my father and I know Jeremiah Wood. Neither of them are going to allow me to escape them. And... who is Aurelia?"

His whole demeanour changes. He grins. "Are you jealous?"

Does he like that I am? I grit my teeth. "Of course not."

His hands come to my biceps and he holds me steady as he presses his mouth to mine. It's like the oxygen is sucked out of the air, leaving me feeling light-headed when he pulls back.

He gives me a smile as his hands move around the back of my neck. "Aurelia is my sister. She was at the church when we got married. She was the dark-haired girl. My brothers are bringing her here. It's safer for you both to be together."

Her image dances across my memory. I remember seeing her briefly. "Was your whole family at our wedding?"

"My brothers were there too, and my father. I should have introduced you to everyone, but there will be time for that. Zeke's wife likes to have us over for dinner quite a bit, so no doubt there will be an invitation extended."

I can't help but think how surreal this whole situation is. I can't deny that I'm grateful the man in front of me is my husband though. I find myself hoping he is not disappointed in me. Am I what he expected?

"But no, it's not your father who has been in touch. It's Wood. He called my mother earlier. Your father is reportedly in surgery. I'm not even sure if he knows the situation."

"He saw me get taken. He knows, though he might not know it was your family who did it."

"I'm sure Wood will enlighten him when he comes to. He seems to be leading this shit."

My stomach rolls.

"Is he coming for me?" My heart stutters and my head starts to feel fuzzy. If he was cruel to me before, I can only imagine how terrible he will be now that I've married some-body else.

Luke moves so he is standing in front of me, his hands coming to my hips. "I'm not handing you over, Sariah. I don't give a fuck what happens. You are my wife, and I won't let him near you. My family can handle Wood. We have allies and support."

He doesn't explain who that support is, but it doesn't matter. His assurance soothes me and makes my fears disappear. "This is a dangerous route you chose to take, Luke."

His smile is lopsided and a little dark. "We like to live on the edge."

My concern must show on my face, because he grabs my hands and squeezes them. "Wood doesn't scare us. He's a back-alley wannabe mobster. His support circle is limited, and that's why he was seeking this alliance with your father. We cut the legs out from under him."

"My father will side with him. He won't like what you've done either."

"I don't want you to worry. It's being handled."

"You asked if it was Declan on the phone. What has he done?"

Luke moves back to the pan. For a moment he doesn't say anything, and I think he's going to keep his silence and his secrets. Then he speaks. "One of our businesses was fire-bombed last night."

My jaw nearly hits the floor. Fear climbs through my veins, reaching for my heart. It finds my stomach instead. I stagger, grabbing hold of the top of the counter to steady my legs, which suddenly feel weak. "Is anyone dead?"

Our actions caused this. We brought this down on our heads—Luke by taking me, and me by agreeing to the wedding. I should have just married Jeremiah and not cared about how I felt or what I wanted. Life isn't fair. I know that first-hand. The thought that people could have died because of my actions makes me feel sick. I place a hand over my stomach, trying to calm my rolling belly.

Luke grabs my face between his hands, cupping my cheeks. He forces me to look at him. "Hey, hey—this isn't your fault. You never threw that petrol bomb into that building. No one blames you."

But he's wrong.

Because I blame myself.

My happiness comes at a price, and I'm not sure it isn't too high of one to pay.

CHAPTER 19

Lucas

I leave Sariah watching TV in the lounge and head to the control room. The room is completely soundproof and has a wall of screens that show every angle of the penthouse. I often thought Zeke was a paranoid bastard. His security system rivals no other I've ever seen, and when I first had taken over his penthouse, I considered getting rid of it. I'm glad I didn't now. I'm able to watch over Sariah as I do what I need to.

I keep my eyes locked on the screen that shows my wife even as I dial Kane. He answers on the third ring.

"How hot are things?" I ask, now that I can talk freely without worrying Sariah.

I need to be involved in what's happening. I owe it to my brothers to have their backs. I don't want to leave my wife, but my family needs me to protect and shore up our defences. I'm not the kind of man who can just sit around and let things happen while I'm ensconced safely in my castle. I like to get my hands dirty and be involved in whatever is happening.

"About as bad as I expected. We put a lockdown on all our other businesses, but I suspect Wood will do more damage."

Kane sounds annoyed. I don't blame him for his frustration. "His retaliation, while not unexpected, changes the playing field."

Just a little bit. I didn't think he would take it lying down, but I didn't expect such a violent payback. I have to admit part of me hoped he would just walk away, concede the defeat, but I understand why he couldn't. Sariah isn't a woman who can easily be pushed aside and forgotten. If I were Jeremiah, I would fight for her tooth and nail.

"So, what's the plan? Tell me Charlotte has one."

"She wants to speak to Declan before she does anything she can't take back. We can't do that until the fucker wakes up from his surgery, and even then it's going to be risky. Wood has men all over the hospital. I'm not looking to get murdered." He blows a breath down the line, and I can sense his irritation. "Charlotte wants me to marry the Adams girl sooner than was discussed. Her father is pushing back. He wants the girl to have the big white wedding. The whole event. I couldn't care less about a fanciful affair, but he won't move forward or help with our situation unless we agree to it."

We have history with the Adams syndicate, and not good history. I'm surprised they would entertain the idea of marrying their daughter to my brother, but old hurts can be forgotten if it furthers a cause. I talk a lot of crap about my mother, but she is the queen of causing shitstorms and smoothing them over. "If you don't marry her soon, there is a risk that they might defect to Easton and Wood's side."

"You think I don't know that?" he snaps. "What would you have me do, Lucas? Short of abducting the girl and forcing her down the aisle, there is nothing."

Considering that's what I had done with Sariah, I don't understand his problem with it. "It worked for me."

"And then we will be at war with the Adams, the

Easton, and the Wood syndicates. Even if we call on the Untamed Sons to stand beside us, we cannot face that many enemies."

He's right. We need to tread carefully and keep our allies closer than ever. "Hamish Adams knows what we've done?"

"He knows. He is fully supportive of the move, hoping we might rid London of yet another family. He'll give us support in exchange for marrying his daughter and some territory he wants that butts onto his own. He also wants a payout, but Charlotte didn't get into the details of what that would entail."

It wouldn't be the first time a syndicate has died a horrible death in London. With the Sons help, we got rid of the Farleys, and before that the Sons got rid of the Blackwoods. Syndicates have a habit of disappearing when they get too big. It's better to be friends with us than enemies.

"How many died in the petrol bombing?" I ask. I need to know what kind of serious situation when dealing with.

"Seven. There would have been more, but the bar had only been open for an hour. Most of the casualties were the bar staff. That cunt needs to die for that."

"Those who died will have their lives avenged. Count on that, brother."

"How's things going between you and the wife?"

I'm not a man who kisses and tells, and what happens between me and Sariah is our business.

"None of your business. I'll be with you in about an hour, so try to stay out of trouble until then. Goodbye, Kane." I hang up the phone knowing my brothers and parents will take care of things while I look after my wife.

I get a message on my phone almost immediately, telling me the doctor's here.

I enable the lift for her to come up. I should have called Mary, the doctor who takes care of things for us usually, but it doesn't feel safe to have strangers know Sariah is here. I called Gemma instead.

I try to leave my cousin out of our dealings as much as possible. It's no secret she hates us, and I don't blame her for that. Anthony did destroy her life, and I know she's never forgiven him for that. Nor should she, but you don't get to pick your family, and she is, whether she likes it or not, a Fraser. That comes with responsibilities.

As a qualified trauma doctor, she has skills we can utilise. Though I usually only call her if someone is missing a limb.

I push up from my seat, stepping back into the living area to go to the door. Sariah's eyes come to mine. She is sitting on the sofa with a blanket wrapped around herself. Fuck, she is beautiful. Her blonde hair tumbles over her shoulders in loose waves, and her now make-up-free face looks so much better than it did with all that shit piled on.

"Is everything okay?" she asks.

"The doctor's here." I walk over to her and sink onto the edge of the sofa. "She'll sort you with the pill as well as anything else you need. Have you made your list of clothes and supplies that you want?"

She nods to the coffee table and the piece of paper sitting on top of it. "I put as much as I can think of."

I kiss her temple, needing to feel close to her. "I will arrange to have that stuff brought here. If you need anything else, we can send out for it."

I twist around as Gemma steps into the foyer area of the apartment. My cousin looks pissed, and I don't blame her. This is beneath her. Mary could have prescribed birth control pills and she could have seen to Sariah's injuries too.

"Somebody better be dying," Gemma says. "I had to leave work for this. I can't keep coming up with family emergencies as a reason."

I should feel guilty for infringing on her life, but I don't. We all have our roles to play, Gemma included.

I kiss Sariah's head again and push up from the sofa. As I approach Gemma, I grab her arm and yank her away from where Sariah can hear us. "Have you finished being a bitch?"

It's the wrong thing to say, because her eyes flame with anger. "Maybe if you didn't treat me like one." It's a fair point. But I don't have time or the inclination to argue with her.

"I need you to take a look at her." I indicate Sariah behind me.

Gemma peers around me to look at my wife before she snaps her eyes back to mine. "I don't see any blood and all her limbs are intact. Please don't tell me you called me away from work for nothing."

I squeeze her arm enough to inject warning into the gesture. Her eyes cloud with pain for a moment before I loosen up my hold. "You are a member of this family, and you will do what is required of you."

Gemma shrinks back a little, even as she tries to steel herself against my anger. I respect her show of strength, even though it's standing between me and getting what I need.

"That woman over there is to be treated with fucking respect. She has some old injuries I need checked out to make sure they're not going to be a problem, and you need to sort out birth control."

"I'm a trauma doctor, Lucas, not a family fucking physician."

"You are whatever I say you fucking are. We all play our part, Gemma. You are not exempt just because you're trying to live a fucking civilian life. You will always be a Fraser."

She grits her teeth and tears free of my grasp. When she raises her eyes to me I can see the anger in them. "Fine. Whatever you need." I don't miss the sarcasm in her words. "Where am I doing this?"

"The guest room at the bottom of the corridor." Clutching her doctor's bag, she storms past me.

I go back to Sariah, who is watching me intently. "She didn't seem very happy."

"My cousin Gemma. She has a penchant for melodrama. She'll take care of you though. Don't tell her who you are."

"Why not?"

"The less people who know you're here, the better."

I wish I could sit in with her, but I think Sariah needs some air to breathe, and she deserves privacy. I get the impression that isn't something she's had a lot of. I put on a fresh pot of coffee and wait while it brews. Once it's done, I pour a cup and sit at the breakfast bar, waiting. I send the list to Talia, my father's assistant. She will know what to get. I've nearly drained the entire mug when the bedroom door opens and Gemma steps out with Sariah on her heels. I don't hear what she says to my wife, but Gemma gives me a glare before she makes her way to the lift. Sariah comes to me.

As soon as she gets close, I pull her against me, turning so she's stood between my legs. My hands rest on her hips, and I feel relief at having her back in my arms again. "Well?" I ask.

"My ribs are bruised, but not cracked or broken. She needs to come back with a prescription for birth control. She doesn't carry it. She seemed a little annoyed at the expectation that she would have. "

"Ignore her. You are not an imposition to anyone."

"We'll still have to use condoms. We have to wait a while before having unprotected..." She looks a little embarrassed before she says, "sex."

I pull her up to kiss her mouth. "Whatever you need," I say.

My phone pings again, telling me I have a visitor. I opened my phone and see that it's my sister. "Aurelia is here."

154

Sariah looks a little nervous at the prospect of meeting my sister properly this time.

"She won't bite. She is your age, so you should have a lot in common."

"I'll take care of her, I promise. I don't know what you have planned, but I just want you to focus on staying safe and coming home."

Her words warm me to the fucking core. The only people who have ever given a shit about me are my siblings. Her recognition that my family is important to me too is a vital component of our relationship.

The lift dings and the doors slide open. Winters steps out, followed by my sister and her guard, Aaron Leep. He is an ugly-looking fuck. It is the very reason he was chosen as my sister's detail.

Aurelia walks towards me, removing her heels as she goes. She tosses them by the console table and continues towards me. "I don't need a babysitter, Luke. I'm quite capable of taking care of myself. I already have Aaron on my heels all day."

I ignore her griping. "Stay with Sariah, and don't leave the apartment until I get back. And do everything Aaron tells you to."

My sister rolls her eyes at me. It's impossible to imagine that her and Sariah are the same age. Sariah has a maturity about her that Aurelia does not.

"Don't be difficult." I turn to Sariah. "You never got a proper introduction, but this is my sister Aurelia. This is Sariah."

My sister gives her smile that is both uncertain and also a little hostile.

"Play nice," I warn her.

Aurelia gives me a smile that does not seem sincere. "Don't I always?"

I don't want to leave them together when my sister is in this mood, but I have no choice. I have to go and I've already waited too long, but I don't want to let go of my wife. The thought of leaving her here alone makes me feel uneasy, even despite the security systems in place. "I need to go." I don't mask the regret in my voice.

"So go. I will be okay."

"No one can get into the apartment without me allowing it. I promise you're safe here."

I press a kiss to her mouth and then I leave.

And it's one of the hardest things I've ever had to do.

CHAPTER 20

Lucas

W inters and I get back into the lift and head down to the foyer. He doesn't say a word, he never does, as he leads me out to the parking garage and into the car. I do notice his eyes are more alert than usual, scanning ceaselessly to make sure there are no surprises.

As I get into the car, I push Sariah out of my head. I need to focus. I peer out the window as the car whizzes through the streets of London. I'm not sure what the retaliation will be for Wood's attack, but irrespective of whether we get Easton onside or not, we had better take a stand against that motherfucker. I don't care what schemes my mother is cooking up. We take that bastard out.

When we pull up into the underground garage at Fraser Holdings, I'm feeling on edge. Just as I'm about to get out of the car, my phone rings. I see Kane's name on the screen and swipe my finger across to answer.

"Where are you?" he demands.

"We just pulled into the parking garage."

"Zeke and I are coming down."

He hangs up and I relay to Winters what is going on. Waiting for Kane and Zeke to appear feels like it takes an age, but in reality, it can't take more than a few minutes. Nathan Ford and Ryan Malone are on their heels, surveilling everywhere. I watch both my brothers approach the car, and my senses start to tingle. Something is wrong. Malone obviously feels the same because his head snaps around as he scans the underground garage, seeking threats.

I barely see the figure pop up between two cars. By the time I register the gun in his hand it's already gone off. The shot ricochets through the concrete structure, sounding louder than it is. I scream something—maybe "No!", but I don't remember—as I reach for the door handle.

Zeke twists and ruthlessly shoves Kane to the floor. Then his whole body jolts as if someone shoved him hard. Confusion washes across his face and panic claws at my guts. He's hit. That bullet found a home. His eyes lift and through heavy lids he finds mine. They flutter closed as he slides forward and sinks to his knees.

Kane reaches him before I do, tugging him into his arms before he can hit the deck. I skid onto the ground, my knees scraping along the tarmac as I reach my brothers.

Gunfire echoes through the garage as Malone, Winters, and Ford fire back at our attacker. I ignore everything but Zeke. His head is rolling from side to side as if he can't keep it upright on his own. There is blood trickling from the corner of his mouth that makes my heart race like an express train.

"Where is he hit?" I snap out the question.

Kane's hands roam over his torso and his palm comes away stained red when he hits the spot high on Zeke's chest. I push his hand against the wound. "Don't let go." Cupping my brother's face, I try to lift his head so that his eyes find mine. They are glassy and pain filled. Desperation claws at me. I won't lose him like this. "Zeke, stay awake."

Words spill from his mouth on a rush of air that I barely understand, but I think he says, "Bailey."

My thoughts scatter as Ryan Malone sinks down next to us. "Fuck!" He hisses as he sees the blood seeping through Kane's fingers. "This place is going to be swarming with emergency services in about five fucking minutes. You wanna catch these pricks? You need to go now. Both of you."

I shake my head, feeling numbness starting to spread through my body. "Not leaving him."

Kane moves aside and lets Malone take over applying pressure to the wound. He grabs my arm and tries to yank me up. "He's right. We have to put an end to this, and we can't do that if we are caught up in the police investigation."

I let him drag me away from Zeke, even though I want desperately to stay with my brother. He needs me—needs both of us. The wound is bad. It's bleeding profusely, and that scares the shit out of me. Malone turns to Winters and Ford. "Keep them fucking safe."

I let Kane drag me into the back of the car, barely focusing on anything as Winters and Ford climb into the front seats with Ford driving. He peels the car out of the garage like we have the hounds of hell on our tails.

Kane peers down at his hands that are covered in blood and shaking a little. I've never seen my brother so out of sorts before.

"Are either of you hurt?" Ford demands, glancing in the rear-view mirror.

I shake my head. "Zeke... Fuck."

Kane's breath starts to rip out of him in heavy pants as his anger grows. "Wood is going to die for this. I'm going to rip out his guts and fucking strangle him with them. You feed him his own fucking heart. I want him dead, Luke. He's got to pay for this."

"And he will."

The car moves out of the garage and back onto the main road. I don't pay any attention. My whole focus is on my eldest brother and what happened to Zeke. Leaving him makes me feel like we abandoned him when he needed us most. It's not a good feeling, but Malone was right. The only way we can exact revenge is not to be caught up in a police investigation. He'll be safe with Malone. I trust him more than I trust Winters.

"We should have stayed with him." Kane wipes his hands on his suit trousers, but it doesn't get rid of the blood.

"We're no good to him sitting at his bedside." It's true, we are not. "We need to be out there protecting our family."

"We already failed on that count."

We drive for a little while until Ford pulls off into an industrial estate. He finds a quiet side road and stops the car. Winters rummages through the glove compartment and finds a bottle of water. He tosses it into the back.

I watch as my brother opens the car door and hold his hands over the pavement so he can wash them. My stomach feels like a ship caught in a stormy ocean. Zeke has to be okay. Not just for us, but because he has two girls at home that need him. Bailey is going to lose her shit when she finds out what happened. She understands this life better than most, having grown up in an MC, but this is still going to gut her.

As Kane finishes washing his hands, his phone starts ringing. Shaking his wet hands, he pulls it out and hands it to me. "I can't speak to him right now."

I glance at the name on screen.

Anthony.

Fuck, our father is the last person I want to speak to right now, but he might know something that can help us find fucking Wood. I swipe the screen and answer the call.

"Is Kane okay?" he asks without preamble.

The question doesn't surprise me. All my father's ever cared about is his heir. He has put all his effort into Kane as his successor and training him to become the head of the family. "It's your other son who is bleeding all over the parking garage."

Anthony sounds impatient as he says, "I already know Zeke is being taken care of. I spoke to Malone. They are on their way to the hospital, and there are police everywhere. It's going to take a fuck of a lot to smooth this over."

My father's politicking doesn't interest me, and I don't care how he gets around the law. My only priority is my brother and whether he's still breathing. He didn't look good when we left him. "Keep me updated about Zeke."

"As soon as I know anything, I'll tell you. This had to be Wood's men."

No shit. "Kane and I will deal with that cunt." I can't stop the rasp of anger that is threaded through my voice. I want to ask if Charlotte is happy she's caused this, but it doesn't matter. The fact is that we are here, and we have to deal with the fallout. "I have to go. Make sure you call Bailey as soon as you know the situation with Zeke." My parents are so wrapped up in themselves I wouldn't put it past them to forget Zeke's wife even exists.

"I'll make sure she's taken care of. Where are you and Kane now?"

"On our way to pay Jeremiah Wood a visit."

"Absolutely not. You come back here and we'll come up with proper plan."

He is deluded if he thinks that's going to happen. "You and Charlotte created this fucking mess. Kane and I will clean it up."

I end the call and hand the phone back to my brother, who asks, "What did he want?"

"To make sure his heir is still breathing." I don't tell him about the rest because there is no point. Kane is never going to side with our father on this. Someone came at our family, and that has to be paid for with blood.

"Fucking prick." Kane lets out a displeased sound from the back of his throat. I don't blame him. Our father has always shown a disregard for the rest of us. None more so than Zeke. "We need to find Wood. We need to bleed that motherfucker dry."

We head to a safe house in the middle of our territory and lay low for a few hours while Parker Weston, Talia's father and Antony's lieutenant, tries to locate where Wood is holed up. Kane sits on the beat-up sofa in the living room, playing absently with a knife while I call around every contact we have.

My phone rings and I answer it. I'm going out of my mind sitting here doing fuck all while Wood runs around free. I'm not a man who is built to sit on his arse. "Speak."

Parker Weston lets out a sigh on the phone before he says, "We found that fucker."

"Where?" I demand.

He doesn't speak for a moment. "Your father has expressly forbid us to retaliate yet."

I let out a string of curses, frustrated more than anything. "Fuck what my father wants. This cunt directly attacked us. The Fraser syndicate is not so weak that it does not fight back when we are attacked."

There is silence again. "I agree. It makes us look like easy targets. But your father was explicit in his command."

"Then give me the details and Kane and I will go ourselves. I will not allow that bastard to get away with hurting Zeke and firebombing our business. The time has come now to show strength."

Weston seems like he wants to give me the information, but he knows my father will be unhappy if he does. Pissing off Anthony Fraser is never a good idea, though Kane and I do it routinely.

Weston reels off an address. "I'm coming with you and I'm bringing men. Your father will be less forgiving of my betrayal if you end up dead."

He hangs up the phone. I grin to myself. I've known Weston since I was a boy. He's been at my father's side forever, one of his most trusted advisers. He is right when he says my father will see this as a betrayal, but Kane and I will protect Weston as much as we can from my father's wrath.

I push up from the table where I'm sitting, my eyes finding my brothers. "Let's go."

Kane and I head out, flanked by Ford and Winters. We need to move quickly, before my father gets wind of what we're doing and puts a stop to it. Adrenaline pumps through my veins as we get into the car and make our way to the address given to us by Weston. Wood is going to suffer for what he's done. If Zeke dies, there will be no place for him to hide.

When we reach the meeting place, Ford puts the car into neutral and pulls the handbrake up. He turns around in the front seat to look at both me and Kane. "You stay close to me and Winters."

If he thinks I'm going to hide behind my bodyguard, he's wrong. I don't need protecting. What I need is to feel the sting of vengeance. Nothing is going to stand in the way of that.

Weston and some of the other men pull up in their cars next to us. Kane and I get out of the back seat and go over to Talia's father.

He eyes us both, as if trying to gauge whether we're level. I'm not entirely convinced I am, so I don't try to hide the anger that is racing through me. "Any news on Zeke?"

I shake my head. During the hours we'd been sitting in the safe house, we hadn't heard anything. I wasn't sure if that was a positive or negative, but the lack of information is starting to piss me off. We should be at the hospital with Zeke, helping him pull through this.

But this *is* helping him. If the roles were reversed, our brother would be here, avenging us. That thought steels my shoulders and relieves some of the tension rolling through my body.

We go over the plan, as rudimentary as it is. Then we attack.

Weston's men enter the bar first, leaving Kane and I outside. I want to be involved in the action, but both of us are too important to risk. Winters and Ford are standing on either side of us, waiting and armed, ready for whatever may come.

Shouts come from inside the building even as gunfire ricochets around. Patience isn't my strongest suit, and I'm desperate to be inside, locating Jeremiah fucking Wood. As I stand there, I imagine the things I'm going to do to him. I'm going to enjoy every fucking second of it. I glance at Kane and see he's getting twitchy too. Like me, he is ready to bring the action.

It feels like the minutes drag on, but in reality it can't take more than five minutes for them to gain control of the bar. When Weston re-emerges from the door, he beckons us forward and we follow him inside.

The club is not high-end. The floors are sticky as we walk across them. There is a bar the length of one wall, and booths line the edges of the room. The smell of stale beer hangs in the air, a sickly, disgusting stench. Men have been bunched together on the floor, facedown, their hands interlinked behind their heads as Fraser men point guns at them.

"Wood isn't here, but we've got one of his high-ranking lieutenants." Weston rubs a hand over his face. "He might be able to give us a location, with the right persuasion."

I know exactly what persuasion he's talking about. It's the

kind that involves knives and flames. It's a punishment that I'm all too eager to dole out. Frustration from the past few days means I'm ready for a fight. My blood heats at the thought of slicing somebody, of making them feel pain. I enjoy the bloodlust, perhaps not as much as Kane, but enough to make me a little bit on the crazy side.

"Bring him to the warehouse. Gun." I hold my hand up for his weapon and Weston hands it to me. I move along the line of men who are facedown on the floor with their hands interlinked behind their heads. Kane moves to the other end, having acquired a gun from someone else.

I give Kane a look, and he nods slightly, telling me he's ready. I cock the gun and I put a bullet in the first man. The back of his head explodes, brain and blood flying into the air. I don't give it a second thought. I move to the next man and pull the trigger again, then the next, going down the line until I meet Kane in the middle. The air fills with the coppery tang of blood, infusing my nostrils. It's a heady scent, and I breathe in deeply. These cunts deserve to die. They picked the wrong side and paid the ultimate price for that. Everyone in this life knows this is how the end may come. We don't fear it but accept it. It is the dangerous line we straddle every day. To be in this life, you have to accept you may not die old in your bed but bloody in the street.

We organise the clean-up with some of our crew and then we head to the warehouse. Both Kane and I are eager to talk to this man, to torture him and find out what he knows. He will either squeal like a pig and give us all the answers we need, or he will take his silence to his grave.

The warehouse is in an industrial estate that has long been disused. It's the main reason we like using it. No one around to hear the screams of our victims.

As I climb out of the car, my adrenaline flares. I'm ready for the upcoming fight—not that this man will fight back. His life was over the moment we took him. The only decision he has now is how easy his end comes.

Kane moves behind me as we head towards the door of the warehouse. I can feel the excitement coming off my brother. Kane lives for the moments like these when he gets to unleash his demons in a controlled way. We all love this, even Zeke. If it were Kane who was lying in the hospital right now, Zeke would be here, ready to dole out retribution on his behalf.

My brother would also make sure I was avenged, and that is exactly what we are going to do. Wood's lieutenant is going to pray for mercy that neither of us are going to deliver.

As we step into the building, the cold air hits us. It's like a fucking refrigerator unit in here, and for good reason. It's harder to think when you're cold. That's what we need. Our victims to be terrified, freezing, and open to talking.

I crack my knuckles as we move into the back room, past the boxes and crates, past the huge storage shelves that are collecting dust. The air smells musty and damp. I can only imagine the fear that man must have felt being dragged through the building, knowing he's in for hours of torture. My brother's reputation in particular is well-known amongst the gang culture.

We step into the room. I can already smell the piss and sweat. It clings to the air, a heavy shroud. The lieutenant is hanging from a hook in the ceiling, his arms stretched over his head so that he is balancing on his tiptoes. I can only imagine the pressure it's putting on his shoulders and the pain he must be feeling down the back of his neck. He is naked, sweat beading on his skin. I'm not surprised to see the defiance shining in his eyes because I would have the same look on my face too. I can tell this fucker is not going to back down easily. I relish the challenge. This is going to be fun.

Weston is leaning against the wall. He pushes up when we

enter and comes over to us. "He hasn't said anything yet. Not that I expect he will without persuasion."

Kane gives a macabre grin. "We'll get him to talk. Don't worry about that."

Weston lets out a breath. "Your father is going to be pissed that we went against him."

"Our father should have been first in line to retaliate when Zeke was attacked." My words come out on an angry hiss. "He was all too keen to be proactive when they wanted to attack Wood. He will just have to deal with what we've done."

"Your father could kill me for what I've done." There is no fear in Weston's voice. Over the years, he's stood toe to toe against my father many times and lived to tell the tale. He is one of the few people who can get away with standing against Anthony Fraser. He and my father have been friends since they were children, and that gives him a certain amount of leeway that other people don't get. He may have pushed it too far this time though.

"We'll ensure that does not happen," I tell him, meaning every word of it. Weston is family, as is his daughter Talia. If my father tries to hurt them, I will stand against him.

Weston doesn't say anything else because there is nothing else to say. Instead, he steps around us and gestures back at the lieutenant. "He's all yours." Kane waits until the door shuts behind us before he moves over to the table of instruments that we can use to gain information from this man.

He picks up a savage-looking knife and twists the blade so it catches the reflection of the bare bulb hanging over our heads. "Do you know who I am?" he asks the man.

"Fuck you." The man spits the words like they are venom.

Kane doesn't show any emotion as he flicks the knife out and tears a long gash down the side of his chest. The blood bubbles and trickles down his skin and I watch it, transfixed.

I move to the table and pick my own weapon, choosing a small handheld blowtorch. Adrenaline pumps through my veins, creating excitement. I can't wait to make him suffer.

"Let's try that again, shall we?" Kane says in an always pleasant voice. That's when he's at his most dangerous. Because my brother is never pleasant to outsiders.

Kane stabs the knife into our enemy's side. The man lets out an uncontrolled wail and throws his head back as he tries to clench his teeth against the pain. He'll find no reprieve though. Neither Kane nor I will give him any.

"Kane.... You are Kane Fraser," he hisses out before his eyes find mine. "Which means you are one of his brothers."

"Lucas Fraser." I give him a beaming smile, enjoying the way he pales at my name. "You're going to tell us where your boss is, or we're going to make you beg for mercy."

He spits in our direction, but it doesn't get close. Disgusting cunt.

"Then I guess we do this the hard way." I moved towards him menacingly and switch on the blowtorch. Then I let my demons out of the box.

"S o, you're my brother's new wife."

I snap my gaze up to meet Aurelia's. I've been busy in the kitchen since she arrived, fixing us both something to eat. I have no idea what to say to her. I've never been good with people, largely because my father kept me hidden for so long, and I'm certainly not good at small talk, though I should be. This woman, who is more or less my age, is my new sister-in-law. I should make an effort to know her, to engage, but in truth, I am terrified of her.

Not because I believe she will hurt me or upset me, but because I want her to like me. I have seen how important Luke's family are to him in the short time I have known him. I want him to see how much his family mean to me also.

"I didn't realise you were in the church. I wish Luke had introduced us properly. But it's nice to meet you now."

"My brother can be difficult."

Her words incite something in me I didn't expect. The need to defend him.

"That's not what I've experienced of Lucas. He's been nothing but good to me."

She tilts her head to the side, and I wonder what her

motive is here. Is she trying to make me say things I can't take back? Is she testing my loyalty to her brother? I have no idea, and that makes me nervous.

"The Fraser men are hot-headed, difficult, impulsive, and a myriad of other adjectives. You need to learn how to control Lucas, or he will control the both of you and you will fade away to nothing. My mother has done this perfectly with my father, and as much as I think my mother is a terrible excuse for human, she is talented in what she does. Make him love you and you will have the power in the relationship."

"You think I need to keep myself protected from Luke?"

"Out of my brothers, he is probably the best. But he still has that dark streak that Zeke and Kane possess. He has Fraser blood pumping through his veins. And that lust for blood is difficult to ignore." She leans forward, clasping her hands together in her lap, her dark hair falling over her shoulder. "You seem like a nice girl, Sariah. Try not to get lost in my brother's shadow."

Neither of us speaks for a while, and she turns the TV on, pulling up some old film that she gets engrossed in. I don't know what to make of Aurelia. Her warning suggests some sort of friendship, but she is still a Fraser, and that means her loyalties lie with her family. Could she be a friend though?

I peer towards the lift where her bodyguard is waiting. Like most of the men who follow the Frasers around, he is intimidating without even saying a word. I'm not sure what to make of him, but I know he scares me less than Winters does. There's something about that man that is off-putting. He looks at Luke sometimes in a way that makes my stomach twist. It's not hate, but it could be close to that. I don't trust him to save his life if it came to it, and it's clear Luke doesn't trust him either.

"Sit and watch the movie with me, Sariah," my sister-in-law says. I give the TV my attention, even though this film is not my kind of thing. Too many car chases and explosions for my liking. I prefer drama, or to get lost in period costumes from another time. I prefer the fantasy of it.

"In the church, it seemed like you knew Luke from somewhere else before you met him at the altar."

I'm not sure if I should talk about my secret, but I don't suppose it hurts for anyone to know how I met Luke. It's not as if my father can punish me any longer or as if I have to hide my transgression from Jeremiah.

"When I learnt I was to marry Jeremiah Wood, I snuck out of my house and went to a club. I didn't want to...." I'm not sure how to explain my situation without sounding pathetic.

Aurelia leans forward and takes my hand in hers. "We are family now. You can tell me anything."

I want to trust her. I've lived a life without trusting anyone for fear of my father and his long arm. He had many spies when I was growing up, and I quickly learnt that people could not be trusted. I want desperately to trust the girl sitting in front of me. I need a friend.

"I went there to lose my virginity so that it wouldn't be taken forcefully from me. I wanted that to be on my terms, to experience it without fear or damage." And I have absolutely no doubt that Jeremiah would have damaged me.

Aurelia cocks a brow and I'm not sure if my words have impressed or surprised her.

"And you met my brother?"

"Luke and I were drawn to each other immediately. He was so gentle, so loving. I don't feel any fear with him."

"So you got quite a shock when you were standing in front of him in that little chapel, ready to be married to a stranger."

"I did. I think he was shocked too. Neither of us knew who each other really was. I used a false name, and I didn't put together that Luke was Lucas Fraser."

Aurelia tosses her hair, drawing her feet underneath her she sits back on the sofa. "Why would you? It's not as if Luke isn't a common name." Her eyes go a little hazy as she stares at nothing. "Soon it will be me standing in a church in front of a man I don't know, taking vows I don't believe in. I think my brothers would protect me from that fate if they could, but we must all play our part. Mine is to provide an alliance with the man of my parents' choosing."

I squeeze her hand, giving her all the strength I possess. "If you don't want to marry, I will help you in whatever way you need help. I know what it's like to have all your choices taken from you, and if you truly do not want it, then I will save you however I can."

I can tell my words have surprised her. Considering everything I've told her, did she expect me to encourage her to do what her family demands?

"I may just take you up on that." She rasps out the words as if she's choked up with emotion.

As I'm about to respond to her, the lift pings and we both glance up as Luke steps off the lift. His eyes are wild, frighteningly so, but it's the blood covering his hands and face that terrifies me the most. What happened to him? It's matted in his hair and splattered up his neck. I can't stop from getting off the sofa and going to him. He looks strung out, though whatever high he's had is not a chemical one. As I get closer, he holds his hands up defensively. "Don't touch me!"

I stop in my tracks, noting the desperation in his tone. Fear makes my chest ache as it heaves to draw in breath. Where has he been? And what has he done? "Luke?"

He's never been like this before. He seems afraid of me.

"I don't want to hurt you."

He takes a step back, putting more distance between us, and my heart squeezes as he does.

"You're not going to."

He shakes his head, as if he's trying to clear the voices whispering darkness in his ears. "Leave me the fuck alone," he hisses and turns towards the bedroom.

I watch him go before turning back to Aurelia.

She shifts her shoulders. "I would do as he says. Give him some time to cool down and he'll be all right."

She goes back to watching the TV as if her brother hasn't just walked in covered in blood and spitting fire. I ignore her. Whatever Luke is going through, he is not doing it alone.

It may be suicidal, but I follow him into the bedroom. He must be in the bathroom, because I hear the shower switch on. Cautiously, I step inside, steam starting to fill the space as the water runs. He's naked under the spray; my eyes can't stop from being drawn to his body. Luke has a good physique; the urge to reach out and touch him is always there. I wait while he sluices the blood off his skin, watching as he scrubs his head and face to let the evidence of his crime go down the drain. I want to ask questions, find out what he's done and whose blood is on him, but I don't want to know either. Ignorance is, after all, bliss. My new husband is a dangerous man, and I knew that before I said my vows. But I've also seen love from him and that changes things dramatically.

My skin starts to feel sticky as the heat and steam from the shower fill the room. I'm glad when he finally switches the spray off and steps out of the shower. He doesn't look at me as he reaches for a towel and wraps it around his waist.

Luke has his back to me, his hands resting on the basin and his eyes locked on the mirror. I don't like what I see. There's an edge to him that's never been there before. I'm not scared, not of Luke, but I do feel a hint of nervousness roll through me. Because this is not the man who left the penthouse hours ago. The man standing in front of me is more beast than man. There's a wildness that I'm not sure how to break through.

"Luke...." I say his name hesitantly, not sure what sort of reaction I'm going to get from him. His eyes lift in the mirror's reflection and find mine. I want to take a step back, but I hold my ground. I won't fear my own husband, even if he's only been that for a short time.

"I told you to leave me alone. I'm not... I'm not in my right mind. I don't want to hurt you." His hands shake, not from fear but from rage. The anger is written in every tense line of his body.

"I'm not scared of you. I'll never be scared of you, Luke. You're a good man."

I take step towards him and he spins. He grabs my shoulders, pushing me against the tile behind my back. I let out an *oof* as pain radiates up my spine.

"I just tortured a man for hours. I cut his skin. I burnt him while he screamed. I carved at him, making him beg for mercy that I never delivered. I enjoyed it. Relished it, even. It made my blood pump and made me feel alive. I live to destroy. It is who I am, what I am. I am poison, a monster in the dark. Do you still think I'm a good man?"

His words make me swallow bile. He is a Fraser, the son of a mob boss. I didn't expect he would be rainbows and unicorns. But hearing his candid words makes a chill run through me. Who has he tortured, and why?

"What happened?" I peer up at him, my heart pounding in my chest, but I'm still not scared. I'm worried for him. He's walking along an edge, and he may drop off it if I don't keep tight hold of him.

"You need to leave. Before I do something I can't take back."

His eyes flash dangerously. Is he still drunk on the blood-lust of what he did?

I shake my head, refusing to leave him trapped inside his own mind with whatever he is dealing with. I recognise the monsters staring back at me because I've seen them in Declan's eyes many times. His temper had terrified me. I don't feel that same fear from Luke. He may be lost in whatever he's feeling right now, but he's not so far gone that he's going to destroy me. "I'm not going anywhere."

I steel my spine, unsure what he's about to do. So I'm surprised when he slams his mouth against mine, devouring me like I'm his reason for breathing. He presses against me, making between my legs throb with need. I don't care that he's fresh from hurting a person. He is my only focus.

He slants his head, taking the kiss deeper until I'm gasping for breath. Then he pulls back, his forehead pressing against mine. "I need you."

I cup his face. "I'm right here. Tell me what happened."

He slams his fist into the wall next to my head and lets out a yell that makes my blood run cold. "They hurt my brother. He's in the hospital. I had to talk to one of his men in an attempt to discover his location." His lips curl into a snarl. "I'm going to hunt down Jeremiah Wood, even if it kills me, and I'm going to put a fucking axe through his heart. He came at my family."

I understand his need to protect. I would feel the same in his situation if I had siblings and people I cared about. Declan isn't my father, so I could have a whole family out there I don't know about. The not knowing is the worst. I hate lying to Luke. He is my husband, and I don't want to start our marriage based on a foundation of untruths. Admitting the truth may make me vulnerable, but better now than down the line when it has the power to wound.

"I'm not an Easton." Saying those words should make my stomach twist, it should hurt, but I actually feel liberated. It's like a weight lifts off my shoulders.

The heat and anger in Luke's eyes fade back. "What do you mean?"

I take a steadying breath before I speak. "My mother had an affair. Declan killed her for it." Tears prick my eyes as I think about my mother's fate and the terror she must've felt as my father stole her life from her. "I have no idea who my father is, but Declan forced me to keep it secret. I was terrified I would end up the same way as my mother, that he'd kill me too, so I kept my silence. It's my biggest regret. The only reason he didn't is because I was useful to him in a way my mother wasn't. So if you're banking on my father wanting to protect me and doing what you ask to save my life, it won't happen. He only cares about saving face, not about me. I'm nothing to him, just the hint of a legacy that no longer exists."

Luke scans my face, and I wonder what is going through his head. Does he see me as expendable now too? Was it a mistake to tell him this? Did he marry me thinking I could be used as a bargaining chip, and now I'm no longer of any use to him? I hold my breath as I wait for his answers.

"I don't care about Declan fucking Easton." His hand goes to my breast. "I want to fuck your pussy."

His hand dips down the waistband of the jogging bottoms I'm wearing and into my underwear. I gasp as his fingers slide to my slick folds and push inside me. His mouth moves to my ear. "I'm sorry, little dove, but this is going to be fast and hard."

My pussy pulses and I nod. "Do it," I command.

He does exactly that. He takes me against the wall of the bathroom before finally carrying me into the bedroom and fucking me harder than he ever has.

CHAPTER 22

Lucas

S ariah is tucked against my side, her legs thrown over mine. Her deep, even breaths tell me she's still sleeping, and I'm loath to wake her. Her revelation in the bathroom last night had surprised the fuck out of me. If Easton isn't her father, then who the fuck is? Somehow, I know my mother will use this against her, so I vow in this moment to never allow my family to know the truth.

I will do whatever it takes to protect my wife, even if it means lying to my family. Because Sariah is fast becoming my family. No one has ever been able to calm me the way she did in the bathroom last night. Her body soothed me in ways I can't describe. I'm still worried about my brother, about finding Jeremiah and destroying him, but I feel focused now, not wrapped in anger. I didn't know a person could do that for me.

She starts to stir, and I brush her hair back from her face so I can see her eyes as they open. She finds me and I see the relief as she takes me in and realises that I'm calm. As angry as I was, I'll never take that rage out on her, and she must know that, considering she talked me off the ledge. She is the only person who has ever managed to do that. Even my brothers struggle to keep me level when I'm out of the box.

"Morning," I say to her. She looks a little surprised and peers around.

"How long did I sleep?"

I kiss the side of her face, needing to feel her close to me. "You were exhausted after I fucked you."

I like the way her cheeks pink at my filthy words. She still has that innocent quality about her, that untouched vibe. She scrambles to sit up, pushing her hair off her face as she does. "How are you feeling this morning?" she asks.

I shift my shoulders. "Better than yesterday, but it doesn't fix things. Kane texted me an hour ago. My brother is still in the hospital, but he is out of surgery. The next few days will be touch-and-go. Jeremiah Wood is still at large. I won't rest until Zeke's attack has been avenged."

She strokes my chest, soothing me. It's like her touch calms all the anger inside me and makes me focus more on what has to be done. I should be out there searching for Jeremiah, but we have some of our best people on it. Until they come through, all there is to do is wait.

I'm not exactly known for my patience.

"Zeke will be okay," she tries to assure me. For a moment it works, and when she presses her mouth to mine I forget about everything but her. "I'm more worried about you right now. Yesterday you were different. I've never seen you like that."

I stroke down her arm, needing to touch her. "This is who I am. I'm a monster, Sariah. I've killed men, hurt them, painted the walls with their blood. I don't regret any of it. The man I killed yesterday to get answers doesn't faze me either. I would kill him a hundred times to protect my family. I'm guessing your father largely shielded you from our world, but it isn't sweetness and light. It is dark and full of horror. If you're wanting me to change—"

She places a finger over my lips, silencing me. "I never want you to change who you are. You can't even if you wanted to. We are who we are."

"Did I scare you?"

She doesn't answer for a moment, and I'm not sure if she's going to. Then she speaks. "You didn't scare me, but I was scared for you. I understand you are a Fraser, and that you have a reputation to live up to, but I don't want to lose you either."

"I'm not going anywhere," I tell her, and I truly mean that. I've had a taste of the good life, and I understand now why my brother will do anything for Bailey and his family. I want to always keep Sariah safe however possible. When this shit is all over, I'm going to make sure she has the best bodyguard I can find. I used to worry about my brothers and my sister, and anything happening to them. I still have those fears, but with Sariah, it's different. I feel this need to protect her from everything.

Even lying here now, my heart is racing as I'm thinking about the things that can happen to her.

The things I might not be able to stop from touching her.

Knowing that she is not Easton's daughter makes me afraid for her. Charlotte thought she might be able to bring Declan back onside because we have his daughter, but that isn't the truth. And from what Sariah has said, it seems unlikely he is going to fight to get her back. The question is, what will he do to her for disobeying him?

He comes for my wife, I will kill him. I'll kill anyone who tries to touch her.

We lie for a little longer until we both shower together. I can't stop from touching her as the water sluices down her body. She is fast becoming everything to me. That scares me.

Caring about people makes you vulnerable, and I'm starting to think there's very little I wouldn't do to keep Sariah safe.

She dresses in some of my loungewear, and I leave her in the kitchen making breakfast. My sister is already awake and watching television in the living room. She gives me a cock of her brow as I step into the room and make my way to my wife. I ignore her. I don't care if she heard us fucking like rabbits last night. This is my home now, and I do what I want within it.

I move over to Sariah and wrap my arms around her from behind. She melts back against me. Fuck, I love the feel of her in my arms. It's like she's the perfect fucking fit. I never realised what my life was missing before Sariah came into it.

"Do you want breakfast?"

I nuzzle my nose into her neck, kissing along the column of her throat as I do. She's beautiful, and mine.

"I'd rather eat you."

She twists to peer up at me, her eyes wide as they dart towards the living area and my sister. But Aurelia is too entranced in whatever shit she is watching.

"Do my words embarrass you, little dove?"

"What do you think?"

"I think you're my wife and I can't keep my hands off you." I don't want to either.

My phone buzzes in my pocket and I pull it out. Winters's name flashes up on the screen. Fucking shitty timing. It could be about Zeke though, so I don't dare ignore him.

I slide my finger across the screen to answer it, giving Sariah an apologetic look as I pull her closer against me. "What?"

"Kane's found Wood. Ford called and said he's gone off after him on his own. He tried to talk him out of it, but your brother couldn't be swayed."

"Fuck!" It's not unusual for Kane to go off half-cocked,

but I'm pissed he's done it without me. I want my vengeance too, and I don't want to visit yet another brother in the hospital. "I'm on my way down. Get the car ready."

As I hang up, Sariah's eyes come to mine. "What's going on?"

I kiss her, soft and wet. I wish we could do more, spend the day in bed fucking each other until we can no longer walk straight, but I have to save my brother from whatever stupidity he's embarking on. "I have to go out for a little while."

Worry crosses her face, and I see the question in her eyes. She wants to know more, and I can't give her that. I expect her to push for answers, but all she says is, "Okay." The trust shining in her eyes makes me choke up. I don't deserve it.

I don't bother getting changed into a suit, staying in my loungewear instead as I grab just my keys, wallet, and a fierce-looking knife. I don't keep guns on the property—too risky. Winters will be armed anyway. I give Sariah a final look before I step into the lift and ride it down to the ground floor. Aaron Leep and Winters are together in the foyer. As soon as he sees me, Winters steps towards me. "Ready to go."

I turn to Aaron. "You stay here and keep an eye on the girls. No one comes in or out. Understand?"

Aaron nods. Reassured, I follow after Winters. My heart is racing as I think about the trouble my brother could have got himself into. Jeremiah isn't going to be merciful if Kane shows up to kill him. Nervous energy zings through my body, firing every synapse as it does. I try not to think about worst-case scenarios and just hope that we're in time to stop Kane from doing something stupid. If anything happens to my brother...

I call Weston from the car and ask him to meet us with men. I'm not taking any chances, and extra manpower is the only way to stay breathing.

After what feels like an age, Winters starts to slow the car. I peer through the window as he pulls onto a side road. There is only one structure at the end of it—a dilapidated red brick building. There are graffiti tags along the wall, and the windows were put in on the ground floor at some point and have been boarded up.

Unease ripples through me, my senses suddenly hyper aware. I've learnt to trust my gut over the years. It's saved my life more times than I can count. Right now, my gut is telling me something is wrong. I climb out of the car, my gaze every-where as I try to figure out what the perceived danger is. I don't see anything untoward, but my senses are still tingling. "This is where my brother is?"

"That's what Ford said." He peers up at the building, and I can see the uncertainty in his face too.

"Did you speak to him directly?"

"No, Aaron did."

As soon as these words leave his mouth the *rat-tat-tat* of gunfire fills the air. Winters grabs my arm and drags me behind the car out of the line of fire. Bullets fly past my head, coming from inside the building itself.

"It's a fucking trap!" Winters hisses. He hands me a gun from the holster on his ankle. "Shoot at anything that moves." He pulls a second gun from the holster under his suit, and we start firing back.

I can't see where our enemies are. I just know they're on the first floor of the building and that they mean to kill us. They've taken out Zeke, incapacitated him, and now they're trying to kill me. Is Kane really in trouble, or was it all part of a ploy to get me here? They knew my weakness exactly and played to it. Like a fool I walked right into the trap. My weakest link has always been my family and the people I care about, and right now it might get me dead.

Sariah's image floats across my mind. Aaron double-crossed us, and he is alone with my wife and my sister. They will trust him because we trusted him. I wonder how long he's been on the payroll of someone else. As soon as I get my hands on him, I'm going to make that fucker wish he had never been born. I'm going to bleed him from every fucking orifice after I've carved his skin off his bones.

We just have to hold on long enough for Weston to get here. I'm grateful as fuck that I had the foresight to call him —that I hadn't gone Lone Ranger. That decision might just save my life and Winters's.

Winters shields me with his body as the gunfire becomes overwhelming. There is no way we can fight this. This is a battle we are losing. When the firing stops, my heart starts to race. They have us pinned down and they know it.

A voice echoes around the courtyard, yelling out, "Surrender and we'll spare your lives."

For some reason, I don't believe him. I wouldn't show my enemy any mercy, and I don't expect they will show us any either.

I glance at Winters. He checks the amount of bullets he's got left in his gun, his mouth turning down. I'm out too. I've been in some hairy situations over the years, but being pinned down without any way to defend ourselves might be the worst.

I'm not scared to die. We all have to meet our end at some point, and with the life I lead, I expected my death to come sooner than for others, but I have to get back to Sariah and my sister. Fuck knows what kind of danger they are in, what kind of stunt Aaron Leep has pulled. I had no idea that fucker was dirty. He played his part of dutiful soldier so well. How long has he been on Easton's or Wood's payroll? How long has he been feeding secrets back to our enemies, and what did they offer him to turn tail and betray his brothers?

None of that matters. The only thing I need to worry about is how to live long enough to save the people I love.

And I do love Sariah. Our relationship might be unconventional. Our beginning might not have been the one most people have. But she is mine, and I will do everything in my power to protect her life. If Wood gets hold of her, there is no telling what he will do to her. That terrifies me in a way I've never experienced fear before.

I glance at Winters. He gives me a look that says this is the end of the road. But I know it hasn't come yet. Weston is on his way. We just have to hold on long enough for him to arrive.

"I know you're out of bullets." The voice taunts us, sounding disembodied as it echoes through the air. It sounds like our attackers are no longer firing at us from the upstairs windows, but closer. They know we're out of bullets. "If you don't come out, we'll drag you out."

Neither of us move, knowing that to step out beyond the car would be a suicidal move, one that would get us both killed. I hear footsteps coming towards us, and the figure rounds the end of the car with a gun pointing at my head. My life doesn't flash before my eyes, or whatever bullshit people think happens when you're staring down the barrel of a gun, but I do see my wife's face. I wish we could have had more time together, longer to know each other, but I know my family will do whatever they can to protect her. Not Charlotte or Anthony, but Kane and Zeke. I make my peace with dying as the fucker standing in front of me smirks.

A loud sound fills the air, and he jerks back as if he has been punched in the head, his neck snapping. A hole in his head is spilling blood down his face in a macabre waterfall. He takes a step forward as more guns fire, ripping through his body. He jerks with every hit before he slides bonelessly onto his knees and hits the tarmac facedown.

I turn around and see Weston and my father's men rushing towards us. Relief floods me, but it's short-lived as the popping sound of gunfire fills the air. Some of the men find their way to me and Winters, protecting us with their weapons. The fire-fight is brutal and brief. My father's men annihilate Wood's crew. They don't give them a moment's reprieve as they mow down every person they can find.

When it's over, Weston comes to my side. He eyeballs me, his gaze trailing over my body. "You hurt?"

I stand slowly, my legs feeling a little shaky. "Not a scratch on me." I pull out my phone and quickly dial my brother. He picks up almost immediately.

"I haven't heard anything. I told you I'd phone you as soon as I do."

I let out a relieved sigh. Kane is alive and breathing, not in danger. "We have a problem. Aaron Leep is a fucking traitor. And he is alone with my wife and our sister. I'm on my way to the penthouse now. Meet us there."

I hang up before he can question me further and turn to Weston. "Follow us back to my penthouse. We've got a fox in the henhouse."

I get back in the car with Winters after brushing the smashed glass off the back seat. "Drive," I order. "Quickly."

The drive across town feels like it takes an eternity. Nervous energy rushes through me and my anxiety is through the roof. I don't fear my own end, but I worry for my sister and my wife. They are not equipped to deal with this life the same way I am, and I know how cruel men like Jeremiah Wood can be. Sariah humiliated him by not marrying him and by taking another husband. He's going to make her pay for that.

When we reach the penthouse, we head up in the lift all together, squeezing as many men as we can into the cart. When the doors open on the penthouse floor, I expect to be met with screaming or gunfire or something. The silence is worse.

As I move into the living area, I can see signs that Sariah and my sister were both here. There are cups on the coffee table, and something is burning in the kitchen. These are the only signs of anything out of place. Winters checks all the rooms while I come to the realisation that there is no sign of a struggle, meaning Aaron walked them out of the apartment. They trusted him enough to go with him. Fuck. My stomach rolls and it feels like my heart has been caved in with a pick-axe. I've never felt pain like it. I rub my chest, trying to disperse the agony working its way through my torso. It doesn't help. I have no idea what Aaron's endgame is, but I can imagine it is nothing good.

I turn to Weston. "Find where that fucker took my wife and my sister and do it quickly. They may not have much time."

I don't care what it takes and what lines I have to cross. I'm getting my wife and Aurelia back, even if it kills me in the process.

CHAPTER 23

Sariah

S omething feels off. Aurelia trusts this Aaron guy, but something about him puts me on edge. He keeps looking in the rear-view mirror as he drives us to meet Luke. Something about it just doesn't feel right. Luke had wanted us to stay in the penthouse, why would he suddenly change his mind?

Things will never be safe out there until Jeremiah is gone. Has my husband killed him already? It doesn't seem possible that in the short time he's been gone he has managed to achieve that goal. I don't doubt Luke's talents or skills, but Wood isn't a man who will be easily corralled.

I glance at my sister-in-law, expecting to see the same unease in her face, but she's just peering moodily out of the window as if she's annoyed about having to leave the apartment. I grab her hand and give it a squeeze, trying to communicate without words what I'm feeling. Her eyes meet mine and I see the confusion cross her expression. I let my gaze slide back towards Aaron before bringing it to her. I don't trust him.

Dropping my voice low, I say, "I don't like this."

Aurelia frowns at me as if I've lost my mind. Why

wouldn't she? Aaron is one of their men, and there has to be a level of trust between her and him for him to be her body-guard. So why are all my instincts fired up? Why am I afraid? "I don't particularly like traipsing across the city either, but you'll come to learn my brother's words are law."

I shake my head. She doesn't seem to understand what I'm getting at, and she certainly isn't feeling the same unease I am. Maybe I'm overreacting, but I lived with a monster for years. I recognise when I'm in the hands of one. Everything about him is setting my nerves on edge. "Something isn't right."

She straightens in the seat, her whole body tensing at my words. "What do you mean?" she demands in a low voice. Aaron's eyes come to the mirror again, so I give him a forced smile until he looks away.

"Why would Luke make us leave the safety of the pent-house? Why would he want us to go to him? None of this makes sense, Aurelia."

She gives me an amused smile. "I trust Aaron. He's been with our family for a long time."

He might have been, but right now I don't trust him at all. I don't say anything else, though, and eventually we turn into a scrapyard. This isn't right. Nothing about this is right.

Aurelia's eyes find mine and for the first time I see uncertainty there. "Where are we going, Aaron?" she asks.

He meets her eyes in the mirror but doesn't answer her question. His attention just goes back to the dirt track leading through the middle of the scrapyard. There are carcasses of cars lining the path, some with their windows still intact, while others are smashed to pieces. The paintwork has corroded on many, leaving behind a metal shell. Fear clings to me, its sticky grasp making it hard to breathe. This isn't right. Luke would never bring us to a place like this.

I try the door handle, tugging at it, but the door doesn't

open. Panic surges through me as Aurelia does the same. Her door doesn't move either. We are trapped in the back of this car as Aaron drives us deeper into the scrapyard. I can't see the road behind us or any sign of civilisation. That doesn't seem like a positive. My heart starts to pound, racing like an express train. Is this where we die? Luke will never know where we are and would never find us in time even if he did.

"Aaron, unlock the door." Aurelia's command should have him jumping to do what he's told, but the guard just ignores her. She gives me a desperate look and quickly pulls her phone from her pocket. She types out a message, though I don't know what she writes or who she writes it to, but I hope it's to someone who is going to save us.

The car stops suddenly and Aaron turns around, pointing a gun in her face. "Give me the phone."

She glares at him, her eyes cold enough to melt the polar ice caps. "My brothers will kill you for this."

"Your brothers are weak. They will fall, as will the rest of the Fraser Empire. Your time in London is over. A new king is taking over."

The panic-stricken look on Aurelia's face does nothing to help my own anxiety. Fear claws up my spine as the car comes to a halt in front of a small hut surrounded by piled up cars. Three men step out of the building and come to the back doors. They look menacing, huge, and grim. I grab Aurelia's hand as they open the door on my side and pull me out. I fight, scratching and thrashing even as I struggle to keep hold of my sister-in-law. Her hand slips from mine as I'm dragged further away and into the hut.

My heart is thundering as I squint against the darkness inside compared to the bright sunshine outside. I'm pushed down to my knees, a crushing hand on the back of my neck stopping me from moving without pain. Aurelia is shoved down next to me.

"Hello, Sariah." The new voice makes my whole body tremble with terror. I peer around my shoulder as Jeremiah steps into the room and comes to stand in front of me.

He is exactly as I remember, bigger even, and angrier. His eyes blaze with fire as he stares down at me like I'm his prize. "Let Aurelia go. She isn't involved in this," I demand.

"You're not in a position to give orders, darling."

"What do you want from me?" I demand, my voice sounding braver than I feel.

"You are a dead man," Aurelia hisses. I want to tell her to shut up, to stop poking the beast.

Jeremiah walks towards her and stands in front of her. He lifts his arm and backhands her so hard she goes sprawling onto the floor. I try to push to my feet to defend her, but the grip on my neck is so tight I can barely move without cutting off my own oxygen. "Jeremiah, please—leave her alone."

He moves back to me, disgust crawling across his face. He grabs my chin between his finger and thumb, his grip bruising as he forces my attention to his. It feels like he's crushing my jaw, and I try not to whimper, even though I want to. "You married the Fraser cunt. You were promised to me, Sariah. You betrayed me by marrying someone else."

He reaches out and cups my breast through my T-shirt. It offers no protection from his grabby touch. Bile climbs up my throat as he gropes me savagely with little thought of how it will affect me. I can hear Aurelia fighting against her captors to try and help me, but I'm transfixed, frozen in place. For a moment I'm back in Declan's house, standing in the living room while Jeremiah touches me against my will. I can hardly think or focus on anything but the disgusting feel of his fingers on me.

No. This isn't like last time. I have a voice now. I am not Sariah Easton, that scared little girl who let others tell her what to do. I am Sariah Fraser, and I will not go down without a fight. I shove Jeremiah's hand away from my breast and meet his gaze with one that is steely. "You touch me again, and I will break every one of your fingers."

He laughs as if I told the funniest joke. I'm aware of his men at my back and the one standing behind him. Aurelia and I are outnumbered. There is no way we can fight our way to freedom, and Jeremiah knows this. That's why my threat is so laughable. I can't even move off my knees unless the grip on my neck is loosened.

"Fraser gave you a backbone, bitch, but I think I preferred you when you were a frozen lump of ice." He leans down, his mouth inches from my ear. "I'm going to fuck you bloody, and then I'm going to do the same to your little friend."

He wraps his fingers around my throat and forces me to my feet. His grip is so hard it cuts off my air for a moment. He moves me over to the desk and pushes me over onto it, my back bowing as he forces me down onto the wood. When he grinds against my pussy, I feel nausea rise in my throat. I will die before I let him take me like this. I slap at his hands as he tries to hold my wrists over my head. I can hear Aurelia screaming my name, but my only focus is on trying to survive whatever Jeremiah is going to do to me. Is he going to rape me in front of all these people? Is he going to take something from me that I can't get back? Is he going to undo me in ways I cannot fix?

He grinds harder against me, letting out a groan. Then he releases his hold on me. "I have the power here. Don't fucking forget it."

He hits me, slamming his fist into my jaw so hard I see stars. I'm used to taking a punch. Declan used to beat me ruthlessly, but now I realise how much he pulled his punches.

Because Jeremiah does not.

It's like being hit with a block of cement. I taste blood in my mouth, the copper tang of it coating my tongue. I feel like my brain has been rattled inside my skull as the skin starts to tighten over my cheek.

I straighten quickly, pulling my T-shirt back into place. My heart is racing, and my stomach churns viciously. I know how bad things could have got in that moment, and I don't know why he stopped, but I'm grateful he did.

My eyes slide towards Aurelia, who is still on her knees. Her chest is heaving with each breath she drags in, and I can see the fear in her eyes. For the first time, she realises her name is not going to protect her. Because I am a Fraser now and Jeremiah would have raped me without a second thought. We are both in a precarious situation, and that terrifies me. I can only hope that Aurelia managed to get the text off to whoever she was messaging before Aaron took the phone from her. That is our only hope.

Aurelia is dragged to her feet, and we are both shoved into a back office. Jeremiah stands in the doorway and stares at me with a disgusting downturn of his lips. He closes the door and I hear the lock engage as he does.

I turn to my sister-in-law and hug her tight against me. I have no idea what Jeremiah is going to do with us and that terrifies me. I just found my life again and am eager to live it. The thought that it could be taken from me makes anger flood my veins. I'm tired of being a pawn in everyone's game. I just want to live my life, have a family, have fun.

"Did you manage to send the text?" I ask in a low voice. I'm not sure if anyone is listening and I don't want our plan to unravel before it's begun.

"I wasn't texting. I was sending an emergency alert. I have an app on my phone and a tracker that allows me to tell my family when I'm in danger. I think they would have chipped me if they could have."

Hope soars within me at her words. "Did you get the alert off?"

She shifts her shoulders. "I'm not sure. I think so. Aaron snatched my phone off me, so I didn't see if it went through completely."

She pulls out of my grasp to go over to the window and tries to yank the board that covers it away from the frame, but it's nailed shut. "My brothers are paranoid about something happening to me. It used to piss me off, but right now I'm grateful for their weirdness."

I can imagine Luke being like that. He is possessive over things that he cares about.

"As well as the emergency alert, I have a GPS tracker embedded in my phone. They'll find us, I promise."

Whether they'll do it before Jeremiah kills us or worse, I don't know. But I keep my negative thoughts to myself. Strangely, I feel the need to protect her from what is happening.

"So, you know who that guy is out there?" Aurelia asks as I sink onto a beat-up sofa pushed against the wall.

I let out a breath, not sure how to explain my situation. "His name is Jeremiah Wood. I was supposed to marry him instead of your brother. He's a little annoyed that never happened."

Aurelia's brows climb up her forehead. "I knew you were promised to another. It was all my brothers would tell me. But you were promised to him? He's so... old."

Not to mention a raging psychopath. "I wasn't keen on the idea."

"I guess everything worked out the way it was meant to. You and Luke are good together."

"I love your brother." As I say those words, I realise how true they are. I do love Luke. I have loved him from the moment I saw him in the club. He treated me like a person. He was the first one to do that in my life, outside of my mother.

Aurelia stares at me. "I can see that. I think he loves you too, even if he is not quite ready to say it yet. I've never seen him like this with a woman before."

Her words warm me. Knowing Luke might feel the same eases some of the pressure in my chest. I married him because there was little choice in the matter, but I also did it because I wanted to.

"Luke will come," I say with so much authority I believe my own words. "Your brothers will come."

"I hope so. For both of our sakes."

CHAPTER 24

Lucas

As soon as the emergency signal activates on my sister's phone, I know we're being lured into another trap. I have no doubt who has my wife and my sister. Jeremiah fucking Wood. That cunt is trying to draw us out by using the only leverage he has. I will kill him a thousand times over if he has laid a hand on her or my sister.

Kane is sitting next to me in the car, playing absently with a knife. He's cutting the edge of his thumb over and over and watching the blood pool and then drip down his hand. I should stop him, but he seems to need the bloodletting, even if it's his own.

We have over thirty men following us, ready to fight. Whatever happens today, we will take out Jeremiah Wood, and then we will systematically destroy his organisation. He has picked the wrong family to fuck with. For daring to touch my wife and my sister, I am going to make him pay.

As we get closer to the area where the GPS went off, I feel calm come over me. I live for the fight. I enjoy it, and I can't wait to dish out retribution on a man who made my wife's life a living hell. Once I'm done with Jeremiah, her father is next.

For every bruise he put on her body, I'm going to visit tenfold on him.

Winters slows the car and I peer through the front windscreen, leaning forward in my seat to get a good look. There is nothing down here other than some junkyard filled with old cars that are rusted and broken.

Winters glances over his shoulder. "We'll check it out."

He cuts the engine and climbs out of the vehicle with Ford on his heels. Kane isn't content to sit, and neither am I. I need to know my family are safe, and I can't do that by sitting on the sidelines. Winters opens his mouth to tell me to stay behind, but I raise my hand, silencing him. "If you tell me to wait in this car, I'll shove my gun down your throat and pull the trigger."

Winters scowls, not fazed by my threat, but he doesn't argue either. More of my father's men gather around us, piling out of vans and cars that were trailing behind Winters. We don't hang about. We begin our attack in earnest. No one wants to give them a chance to escape or hurt the women. I notice Ryan Malone, Zeke's bodyguard, is also amongst the men. When this is over, I'm going to have words with the man. He's supposed to be guarding our brother.

We move through the graveyard of cars, some piled high enough to provide cover. I still have the gun Winters gave me, though I have fresh bullets for it now. I also have a couple of wicked-looking knives hidden on my body in case I need them. As we move through the maze of broken-down cars, the smell of old engine oil thick in the air, I hear voices.

Malone holds up a hand, stopping us in our tracks as he hides behind the tail end of a car. He peers around the edge as we come to a halt and then turns back to us. "There are ten men guarding what looks like a small cabin. I'm guessing the girls must be inside."

I don't allow myself to think they might have been moved since Aurelia sent the SOS message to us. I don't allow any fear to creep into my consciousness because my sister and my wife need me to be strong.

Malone gives me a look. "Ready?"

I nod and feel Kane moving up behind me, ready for whatever is coming. The men move quickly and attack with precision. I shoot as I move, making a beeline for the cabin itself. I don't care about the men outside. All I give a fuck about is finding my wife and my sister.

As I approach the steps that lead up to the cabin, a man comes at me with a knife. I see the glint of metal as it strikes towards my face. I raise my hands instinctively to protect myself and feel fire down my arm. I barely pay it any attention as I grab his wrist and twist as hard as I can. It takes a couple of goes to get him to release the weapon, but as soon as he does, I slam my own knife into his chest. Blood bubbles on his lips as his mouth moves soundlessly. I push him back, sliding him off the knife, and he goes down to the ground like a sack of bricks.

As I rush up the stairs and tear the door open, a bullet flies past my head so close I feel the breeze against the side of my ear. Fuck, that was close. I rush into the room as two men barrel towards me. A gun explodes behind me, hitting the first man in the forehead. I don't need to twist around to know my brother is at my back. Kane is always wherever I need him to be.

I stab the other man in the throat, tearing the blade out. Blood spurts like a geyser from his neck. Bright red. It stains everything it touches. He slams a hand around the wound, but it pours through his fingers. I don't stop to watch him die, instead moving through the small space towards a closed door at the back. I twist the handle, and as I do, bullets punch through the wood. I recoil to the side, avoiding the trajectory as the frenzied attack continues. There are more of my father's men in the cabin ensuring our safety. All of the men are subdued or dead, leaving me to focus solely on what lies behind the door.

I wait until the firing stops, not sure if the shooter is reloading or if he is out. I risk everything, lifting my foot and slamming it against the wood. The first kick doesn't shift the door. So I kick it again. This time the frame is obliterated and the door swings open.

I expect to be looking down the barrel of a gun, but as I step into the room, I'm greeted by the sight of my wife being held at knifepoint by Jeremiah Wood. My sister is sprawled on the floor, her head tipped to the side, her eyes closed, and her mouth slack. Her face is red, as if she's been hit. I'm going to kill this fucker, slowly and painfully. Malone moves to her side, slow and careful so as not to spook Jeremiah. He goes down onto his haunches in front of my sister.

I don't meet Sariah's eyes. I'm too scared to look at her. If I do, I will break, and I need to be strong for her right now. Kane moves in behind me, pointing his gun at Jeremiah's head. He is flagged by Malone, Weston, Winters, and Ford.

Each man is pointing a weapon at Jeremiah. Sariah's head is tipped back to accommodate the blade pushed tightly against her throat. For the first time in my life, I feel bone-crushing fear. One slip is all it would take to end her life. I hold my breath, hardly daring to draw in air. My lungs feel tight, like elastic bands are tied around my ribs. "Let her go."

Jeremiah laughs, a dark, disturbing sound. "Since she's my only leverage, I think I'll pass."

"Letting her go is the only way you leave this room breathing."

"And then you'll just torture me. I'd rather die. I think I'll take your pretty little bitch with me."

He pushes the blade deeper into Sariah's neck, making her whimper. Blood trails down the column of her throat, a slow roll of crimson. My heart starts to pound in my ears as my rage intensifies. I want to kill this cunt. I want to rip his heart out and bathe in his blood. He is right about one thing. We are going to torture him if he lives. I'm going to strip the flesh from his bones while cutting out his intestines. We will make an example of him for daring to come at us, but for me, there is more to this. This is personal. He touched what belongs to me, because Sariah Fraser is mine, and anyone who dares to touch her will die.

"Oh, you're going to die," Kane says in a dark voice. "You came at the Frasers. That's not something we can just forgive and forget. Your life was forfeit the moment you hurt Zeke. You cemented your death further by firebombing our property. Taking our sister and Lucas's wife means you have no chance of walking out of here breathing."

Jeremiah's eyes snap to mine. "You accuse me of crimes against your family, but you stole the woman I was meant to marry and made her your own. You created this war between us. Do you really expect me to just walk away as if nothing happened? Would you?"

I wouldn't. I would do exactly what he has done. Probably worse. But that isn't the point. I don't care that I would have reacted in the same way. He came at me and mine and he will pay for that.

"Now you're going to let me and this bitch walk out of here. If you come close or try to stop us, I will kill her."

He is bluffing. He needs her alive to escape the situation. However, we don't need him breathing. As he shifts towards the door, a gunshot rings out. Fear clamps around my heart. Who fired, and who was shot? It takes my brain a moment to catch up and see the blood trickling from a hole in Jeremiah's forehead. It takes me a second longer to see my brother,

Kane, with his gun raised in Jeremiah's direction. He took the shot.

Jeremiah staggers and goes down hard, taking Sariah with him. For a moment I worry she's hit too. My legs move before I realise what I'm doing. I drop down next to her, my knees slamming into the wood beneath me. Jeremiah's body is on top of her, and he is heavy to move. Winters is suddenly at my side, helping me lift his dead weight off her. When we get him onto his back, his eyes are glassy, staring unseeing at the ceiling. There is no life in him.

I ignore Jeremiah Wood and give my attention to the downed body of my wife. There is blood on the back of her neck, staining her T-shirt. She starts to move slowly and relief washes through me like a tidal wave. I skim my hand over the back of her body, checking for injuries, but I find nothing. I flip her over and her eyes find mine. Tears overflow, streaking down her cheeks. I gather her into my arms, pulling her against my chest as that ache in my torso starts to loosen. She is safe, she's breathing, and she's back in my embrace.

I inhale her scent, nuzzling my nose into her hair. My heart finally starts to calm itself, and I take a free breath. I pull back, cupping her face in my hands. I notice the bruising starting to mottle her skin and my anger flares. If Jeremiah wasn't lying there dead, I would torture the fuck out of him. "Are you okay?" I ask.

"I knew you would come." The unshakeable faith she has in me awes me. I have never been someone's saviour before, but right now I am hers.

When I pull free, I rest my head against hers with my hand still locked on her face. I need the connection to her. The thought of letting her go fills me with unease.

"Is Aurelia okay?" she asks. I notice she's studiously avoiding looking at Jeremiah's body. I move us so I'm shielding her from him.

I glance towards my brother who is kneeling over our sister. She is starting to rouse, and both Kane and Malone are helping to sit her up. "She's okay."

Sariah clings to me, her fingers fisting my T-shirt. "I thought I was going to die."

"I would never allow it." I kiss her head, needing to feel close to her.

She peers up at me. "All I could think about when that knife was pressed to my throat is that I never got the chance to tell you how I really feel. I love you, Luke. I don't expect you to say it back, but I never want to be in that position again without you knowing the truth."

Her words floor me. I don't expect such candour from her. I realise I feel the same. When you know, you know. Sariah is all I need, and all I want.

"I love you too. I've loved you from the moment I saw you in Tease, looking lost and out of place. I swear, Sariah, I will never let anything touch you again, and the people who were involved in taking you and my sister will pay for their betrayal."

And I mean every word of that. I'm going to make it my personal mission to hunt down Aaron Leep and eviscerate the fucker.

I help Sariah to her feet and then I carry her bridal style out to the cars. She nuzzles against me, and I love the feel of her in my arms. I put her in the back of the nearest vehicle and tell her to wait there while I head back to my brother. Malone is helping my sister to her feet, and I wait for him to take her away before I turn to Kane.

"Aaron Leep is mine."

Kane stares at me. "Why do you get to have all the fun?"

"Because he took my wife."

"And our sister."

"I want him dead, and I want to be the one to do it. I've never asked you for anything, Kane, but I'm asking for this."

My brother looks at me as if he is contemplating telling me to get fucked. Then he sighs. "I want to play too, but you can have first go at him."

It's a compromise and one I'm willing to live with. I find Weston and get him looking for Aaron Leep. I check my sister where she is sitting in the back of the car with Ryan Malone, something I should probably question, and if I was in my right mind I might have done. Then I take my wife back to the penthouse.

After I clean her up, washing every inch of her skin to remove the blood from her, she makes a beeline straight for the sofa and sinks onto it as I drop my keys and wallet on the edge of the countertop. "Do you need anything?"

She shakes her head as she drags a blanket off the back of the chair. "I just want to sleep." She taps the seat next to her. "Sit with me."

I oblige, sinking down next to her and pulling her against my chest. She told me she loved me, and I gave her the words back, meaning it with every fibre of my being. I do love her, and I will do whatever I must to keep her safe.

Including taking Aaron Leep's life.

We put on a film and sit clinched together while it plays. I don't watch it. My thoughts are on what I'm going to do to the man who took my wife and handed her over to my enemy. Aaron was someone we trusted. He was in a position of power as my sister's bodyguard. I wonder how long he has been on someone else's side. How deep his betrayal runs.

I pull the bracelet out of my pocket and peer down at it. I have carried it with me since that night she left it in the hotel room. I don't want to give it back. Having it on my person makes me feel close to her, but it's time. I have her. I don't need fucking trinkets anymore.

She glances up as I hold it out to her.

"I thought I lost that."

"You left it in the hotel."

Her brow furrows. "You kept hold of it all this time?"

I'm not sure how to explain it without sounding like a lunatic, so I shrug. "I liked having a piece of you with me."

Her expression softens as she takes the bracelet from me. "It was my mother's."

Guilt claws at me that I kept it this long. I brush her hair away from her face and kiss her forehead. "I shouldn't have kept it."

She shakes her head. "It's okay. Thank you for returning it."

I pull her against me and listen while her breathing starts to even out. I never thought I could find such peace just sitting with someone. Usually, my peace comes from violence. That has been the only way to soothe my broken soul.

My phone vibrates on the arm of the chair next to me. I move carefully, realising my wife is still asleep, and I pick up the handset. Charlotte's name flashes on the screen. The last person I want to speak to is my fucking mother. I consider letting it go to voicemail, but she'll just keep calling.

I slide my finger across the screen and take the call.

"When, precisely, were you going to tell me that one of our men betrayed us?" she demands, sounding ticked off.

"There wasn't exactly time to call a family fucking meeting," I snap at her. I'm not in the mood for Charlotte's shit right now.

"I am still the head of this fucking family, and I deserved to know."

Anthony might think he runs the family, but clearly Charlotte doesn't agree. We all know she wears the trousers, but though she dictates to my father which way things should go, it's always sobering when she actually admits it.

"You know now."

"Whatever you're planning, I want to know."

"The man took my wife. This is between me and him. Don't get in my way, Mother."

Before she can argue further, I hang up the phone. It starts to ring almost immediately. I think it's Charlotte until I see Kane's name flash on the screen. I answer quickly. "What do you know?"

"Weston picked up our package twenty minutes ago. Come to the warehouse." He hangs up without saying anything further.

I carefully detach myself from Sariah. I gently lay her down on the sofa, covering her with a blanket, and then I leave. Winters insists on coming with me, even though I want to leave him behind to guard my wife. I need to get her security as soon as possible. I know she will be safe in the penthouse. The only reason she wasn't before is because of Aaron's duplicity.

As Winters pulls the car up outside the warehouse, righteous anger starts to attack my gut. I can't wait to get my hands on that prick. I'm going to bleed him, carve at him, take all the anger I'm feeling out on his body.

Winters enters the warehouse before me, and I trail after him. When we get inside, I can smell the sweat. Kane better not have started without me. Not after he promised. As I step into the kill room, I see Aaron is tied to a chair. His head is bowed, his chest bare. He has trousers on, they have been cut up the legs. Though hurt, he looks whole. Good. Kane kept his promise.

My brother is leaning against the wall behind me and gives me a slight inclination of his head as I move further into the room. Red films my vision as I take in the man who betrayed us. When I step in front of him, Aaron raises his head and peers up at me. There is no fear in his eyes, despite the pain he knows I'm going to inflict on him.

"Why?"

Aaron shifts his shoulders. "Wood promised me things you could never deliver."

I slam my fist into his face, making his neck snap to the side. "You disloyal bastard."

All my rage, all my fear, explodes out of me. I beat the fuck out of him, my fists flying as I slam them over and over into his face and body. I want to inflict as much pain as I can. I want him to feel what I felt when I learnt about his betrayal.

Breathless, my knuckles burning, I step back and take a look at my handiwork. His face is swollen, his eyes already puffy. I pick up a knife from the table next to the chair and slam it into his thigh. He screams, a high-pitched wail that makes me smirk. Then I start to carve his legs up. I pull his skin back as I detach it from his muscles. He screams through the whole process, thrashing against the ropes holding him to the chair. I don't give him a moment of reprieve. All I can think about is my sister lying unconscious on the floor of the cabin and my wife with a knife held to her throat. It fuels my anger and makes me feel deranged.

I get bored of the knife and pick up the blowtorch. It is one of my favourite instruments to use in torture. I light it up and then I push the flame against his chest. His shrieks ring out, a symphony that eases some of the tension in my chest. The smell of burning flesh fills the air, a sickly scent that would be repulsive if I wasn't so focused on what I'm doing. He begs me to stop, pleads with everything he has. I ignore him. Betrayal is not something that can be forgiven. If he wanted more, he could have talked to one of us. We would have accommodated him. Instead, he handed my family over to our enemies, and that can't be forgiven.

I torture him until his head is hanging low down on his

chest and his breathing is rapid and shallow. I step back and Kane comes forward. He takes the knife out of my hand, and I let him, too exhausted to argue.

"Now it's my turn."

And as much damage as I thought I inflicted on Aaron Leep, Kane does worse.

Epilogue

SARIAH

ONE MONTH LATER...

L uke is crushed against my body when I wake. He's snoring softly, his face more peaceful than it is when he is awake. I trace circles on his chest, feeling at ease for the first time in my life. I know my husband is not the poster child for good behaviour, but it doesn't matter to me. I don't care if he's a criminal, if he's hurt people, even killed them. When it mattered, he was there to save me, to protect me from a man who wanted to harm me. That is all I ever wanted in life. Someone to care.

I lie quietly for a while, just drinking in the quiet with him, until he starts to stir. I watch as he slowly comes round, dragging himself out of sleep. When he fixes his bright blue eyes on me, I melt a little. My husband has the power to render me speechless with just a look. He's so handsome, although I might be biased.

"Have you been awake long?" he asks in a sleepy voice.

"Not long."

"Now that I am awake, I want to feel your pussy wrapped around my dick."

My body heats at his words. I love when he talks dirty to me. I forget that we have places to be, that we're going to be late to Kane's wedding. My focus is on my husband.

He slips his hand between my legs, and I let out a moan. His touch is like magic, and he knows exactly where to put his fingers for maximum pleasure. Just as he slips inside me, my phone on the bedside table starts to ring.

"Ignore it," he commands as he finger fucks me.

I do as he says, focusing on the sensations growing between my thighs. The phone stops ringing and instantly starts up again. I drop my hands over my face.

I start to roll over to grab my phone, but Luke stops me, holding my hips steadily in place. "They'll wait. This won't."

"What if it's important? What if someone needs help?"

"Then they'll phone back later."

He latches his mouth over my nipple, and I let out a whimper as my pussy throbs. The phone stops ringing and then starts again. This time, I push Luke away and reach for the phone. He lets out an irritated growl as I glance at the screen. Unknown number. Normally, I wouldn't answer. The persistent calling makes me intrigued to know who might be on the other end, so I swipe the screen.

"Hello?"

"Sariah."

I sit up, jackknifing in the bed. My heart thuds. "Declan...." I seek out Luke, who stiffens at the name. There is no love lost between him and the man I used to call my father. I know Luke despises him for what he's done to me, for the pain he put me through and the way he treated me for my mother's transgressions. "I'm surprised to hear from you."

"You've left me nearly a hundred voicemails. You were getting hard to ignore."

He is exaggerating. I haven't left that many, though there have been a few. After Jeremiah died, my father suddenly changed his mind about standing against the Frasers. I think on some level he knew he couldn't defeat them without Jeremiah's support, and the Wood syndicate, leaderless, was in no position to give him any help. From what Luke has told me, they are in a civil war, fighting amongst themselves over who will take the leadership. Luke is happy about this because it keeps them out of the city and focused on their own problems.

"If you answered the first one, I wouldn't have had to do that." My pointed response earns me a cluck of his tongue.

"The Frasers know you are not mine, don't they?"

"Only Luke." He refuses to tell the rest of his family, unsure what danger that might place me in, if any. His mother is a first-class meddler. I learnt that within a week of being in the family. If she knew the truth about my parentage, I think Luke is worried she might try to use it against me somehow, or to their advantage. He's not willing to allow that to happen. He is always protecting me, even from his own family.

"Do you plan to keep it that way?"

"As long as you give me the information I want. Tell me who my father is."

There is a long pause—so long I think the call has dropped. Then Declan speaks again. "Alice never mentioned who your real father was, so I can't help you with that."

Disappointment floods me. I'd hoped I would get answers, that Declan would know the truth. "Then I'm under no obligation to keep our secret."

"Hang on a second," he snaps. "You don't get to defy me. I raised you. Gave you a home. I took care of you."

"You abused me and made my life a misery. You tried to force me to marry a man twice my age who also wanted to abuse me. I don't owe you anything. You're lucky I haven't sent my husband after you to put a bullet in between your eyes for what you did to me and to my mother. Can you get the information or not?"

I can imagine the anger on his face as he takes my words in. It feels liberating as hell to finally be able to stand up to him. I used to fear him, but now I just feel sorry for Declan. He is a sad, lonely, old man, and he will remain that way. He could have made different choices, and we could have been a real family. Blood doesn't define parentage, but he made it a huge deal. Now, he has no one. Not even his syndicate. In a bid to protect some of his holdings, he struck a deal with the Frasers. It made him a servant in his own kingdom, one who answers to Charlotte and Anthony. It's a bittersweet outcome, and I can't say I'm sorry that he has fallen so far. Declan deserves everything he's got.

Worse, in fact.

I thought the Frasers let him off fairly easily. The only reason they didn't dismantle his organisation completely was because he never actually took a stand against the family. Had he done that, things would have been very different.

"Give me time and I'll have an answer for you."

"I'll give you a month. After that, I'm telling everyone." I end the call and slide my phone back onto the bedside table.

Luke instantly wraps his arms around me, pulling me against him. "He'll give you the answers you want. He won't want the secret of your parentage to come out. Declan Easton is a proud prick."

Luke is right. Declan will not want it to come out and embarrass him.

"Anyway, I don't want to talk about Declan fucking Easton. I want to make my wife come."

That's precisely what he does. He fucks me hard until I explode with desire.

Eventually we have to get out of bed and get ready. We shower together and then I pull on my dress while Luke puts on a suit. I'm just brushing out my hair when he comes to stand behind me, his hands going to my shoulders. "I'm not expecting trouble," he says, "but I want you to stick as close to me as you can during the ceremony."

I turn to look at him, searching his face and seeing nothing apparent in his expression. Even so, I feel a hint of anxiety ripple through me. "The fact that you're saying that suggests you are worried. Do you think her family are going to renege on the deal?"

Luke shifts his shoulders. "When it comes to mob weddings, nothing is ever straightforward. The Adams syndicate wants this marriage to go ahead, just as we do. But these things have a mind of their own." He kisses the top of my head. "I would rather you stay behind, in safety, but it will look weak if you do. We must present a united front."

I place my hand over his on my shoulder and give it a gentle squeeze. "It'll be okay. Everything will go off without a hitch, you'll see."

"I hope you're right," he says. "You look beautiful, little dove."

I give him a sultry look. "You scrub up pretty nicely yourself, Luke."

He raises my hand to his mouth and kisses the back of my knuckles. "Let's go and watch my brother get married."

And hope to fuck it won't be a red wedding.

Get a free book and exclusive content

Dear Reader,

Thank you so much for taking the time to read my book. One of my favourite parts of writing is connecting with you. From time to time, I send newsletters with the inside scoop on new releases, special offers and other bits of news relating to my books.

When you sign up, you'll get a free book.

Find out more here:

www.jessicaamesauthor.com/newsletter

Jess x

Enjoyed this book?

Reviews are a vital component in any authors arsenal. It enables us to gain more recognition by bringing the books to the attention of other readers.

If you've enjoyed this book, I would be grateful if you could spend five minutes leaving a review on the book's store page. You can jump right to the page by clicking below:
https://books2read.com/The-Ties-That-Bind

Also by Jessica Ames

Have you read them all?

UNTAMED SONS MC SERIES

Infatuation

Ravage

Nox

Daimon

Until Amy (Until Series and Sons Crossover)

Levi

Titch

Fury

Bailey

Stoker

Cage

FRASER CRIME SYNDICATE

Fractured Vows

The Ties that Bind

A Forbidden Love

UNTAMED SONS MC MANCHESTER SERIES

Howler

Blackjack

Terror

IN THE ROYAL BASTARDS SERIES

Into the Flames

Out of the Fire

Into the Dark

IN THE LOST SAXONS SERIES

Snared Rider

Safe Rider

Secret Rider

Claimed Rider (A Lost Saxons Short Story)

Renewed Rider

Forbidden Rider

Christmas Rider (A Lost Saxons Short Story)

Flawed Rider

Fallen Rider

STANDALONE BOOKS

Match Me Perfect

Stranded Hearts

About the Author

Jessica Ames lives in a small market town in the Midlands, England. She lives with her dog and when she's not writing, she's playing with crochet hooks.

For more updates join her readers group on Facebook:
www.facebook.com/groups/JessicaAmesClubhouse

Subscribe to her newsletter:
www.jessicaamesauthor.com

facebook.com/JessicaAmesAuthor
twitter.com/JessicaAmesAuth
instagram.com/jessicaamesauthor
goodreads.com/JessicaAmesAuthor
bookbub.com/profile/jessica-ames

Printed in Great Britain
by Amazon